Rocky Mountain
BRIDES

Three sisters coming home to wed!

Among the breathtaking landscape and
tranquil beauty of the Rocky Mountains lies the small,
picturesque town of Destiny. It was in this bustling
community that the three beautiful
Keenan sisters were raised, until college and
work scattered them around the globe.

Now Leah, Paige and Morgan are home—
finally reunited—and each with a story to tell....

*Join the sisters as they each find the one great love
that makes their life complete!*

In April we met Leah in
Raising the Rancher's Family

Paige returned home in May!
The Sheriff's Pregnant Wife

Now, this June, get to know Morgan a little better....
A Mother for the Tycoon's Child

Morgan felt a rush of excitement. She wanted to be the woman he wanted...he needed.

Justin arched an eyebrow. "You run a town, you own a business and you're going to head a large development project, and you're telling me you can't give me one little kiss?"

She didn't answer.

"Just tell me this, Morgan. Do you want to kiss me?"

Her heartbeat shot off, pounding. "Yes...."

"Show me," he challenged in a husky rough voice. "I'll sit here. I won't even put a hand on you."

She tried not to be affected, but felt the pull.

"I dare you, Morgan. I dare you to kiss me."

She took the first step, then the second, and realized she had to keep herself from going too fast. "This is crazy."

PATRICIA THAYER

A Mother for the Tycoon's Child

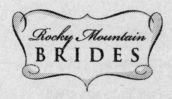

Rocky Mountain
BRIDES

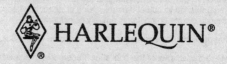

HARLEQUIN®

TORONTO • NEW YORK • LONDON
AMSTERDAM • PARIS • SYDNEY • HAMBURG
STOCKHOLM • ATHENS • TOKYO • MILAN • MADRID
PRAGUE • WARSAW • BUDAPEST • AUCKLAND

ISBN-13: 978-0-373-03955-5
ISBN-10:   0-373-03955-7

A MOTHER FOR THE TYCOON'S CHILD

First North American Publication 2007.

www.eHarlequin.com

Printed in U.S.A.

Patricia Thayer has been writing for over twenty years and has published thirty books with the Silhouette and Harlequin Romance® lines. Her books have been twice nominated for the National Readers' Choice Award, the Book Buyers' Best and a prestigious RITA® Award. In 1997 *Nothing Short of a Miracle* won a *Romantic Times BOOKreviews* Reviewers' Choice Award for Best Special Edition.

Thanks to the understanding men in her life— her husband of over thirty-five years, Steve, and her three grown sons and three grandsons—Pat has been able to fulfill her dream of writing. Besides writing romance, she loves to travel, especially in the West, where she researches her books firsthand. You might find her on a ranch in Texas, or on a train to an old mining town in Colorado, and this year you'll find her on an adventure in Scotland. Just as long as she can share it all with her favorite hero, Steve. She loves to hear from readers. You can write to her at P.O. Box 6251, Anaheim, CA 92816-0251, or check her Web site at www.patriciathayer.com for upcoming books.

And don't miss Patricia's next book
out early in the New Year…
This is one rugged rancher
you won't be able to resist!

CHAPTER ONE

THERE was no sign of him.

Morgan Keenan stared out the bay window of her craft shop at the family Inn, willing the tardy Fortune 500 corporate CEO to appear. Not that she didn't realize what a long shot it was to get Justin Hilliard to even consider investing in her project.

She glanced up at the clouds gathering over the San Juan Mountains, knowing the forecast was for snow flurries later tonight. It was still early in the season, but it could be a blessing for the old mining town of Destiny, Colorado. Especially when she was trying to promote the perfect location to build a ski resort.

Since being elected mayor last year, Morgan had worked hard, pulling together a cost effective package and looking for investors. She'd received a few nibbles over the previous months, but it hadn't been until she heard from Justin Hilliard of Hilliard Industries, that she thought she just might have a chance to pull off this deal.

And today, the CEO was coming to see the town…and to meet her. Or was he?

With one last glance at the empty parking lot, Morgan walked to the back of the craft shop she ran in her parents' bed-and-breakfast, the Keenan Inn. A wooden quilting frame was set up in the turret-shaped alcove. She took her seat facing the windows so she could keep an eye out for her visitor while relieving tension by working on the wedding quilt.

Morgan picked up her needle and took a measured stitch, a skill her mother had taught her years ago. It had been her salvation too many times to count. Lately the resort deal had been heavy on her mind, but after today, if Mr. Hilliard decided he wanted to invest in the resort she could breathe easier.

Busy with her intricate work, it took a while for Morgan to realize she wasn't alone. She glanced up to see a small dark-haired girl standing in the doorway. Dressed in a pink nylon ski jacket and matching bib overalls, she was too cute.

Morgan smiled. "Hi."

The girl didn't answer.

Since the Inn's guests didn't usually have children, Morgan decided the girl belonged to a day tourist. She glanced toward the front of the shop but didn't see anyone around.

"I'm Morgan," she said. "What's your name?"

"Lauren," the child answered softly.

"Pretty name. Do you want to see what I'm making?"

Her gray-blue eyes widened, then to Morgan's

surprise, the little girl walked to the edge of the stretcher board.

Morgan ran her hand over the multiblue patterned fabrics already sewn into circles. "It's called a wedding-ring quilt. See the circles?" She outlined one with her finger. "They look like rings."

The girl didn't speak, but leaned in to look at the half-finished quilt.

"I like to use blue," Morgan continued. "It's my favorite color. What's yours?"

Those big eyes rose to hers. Morgan felt a tug at her heart. "Pink…" the girl whispered.

"You want to see if we can find pink in the quilt?"

Surprisingly the little girl raised her arms to Morgan. She didn't hesitate to lift the child. A soft powdery smell emanated from her as she was tucked perfectly onto Morgan's lap. Morgan took a moment to savor the rare gift, because this would be as close as she would ever get to having a little girl of her own.

Justin Hilliard stood at the Keenan Inn's front desk. He hated being late. Punctuality had been a discipline drilled into him throughout his life. Even if it couldn't be helped because the company jet had a minor mechanical problem, and Lauren had fallen asleep. He'd decided that she needed the rest more than he needed to be on time.

"Sorry for the delay, Mr. Hilliard." The middle-aged innkeeper had short gray hair and warm hazel eyes. "We put you in the suite on the second floor.

My husband is bringing in a rollaway to accommo-
date your daughter."

"Thank you, Mrs. Keenan. I apologize for not in-
forming you ahead of time."

"It's not a problem at all." The older woman
smiled. "We've all been looking forward to your
visit but especially, my daughter, Morgan."

He checked his watch. He was ninety minutes late.
"I was to meet with her today. I'm going to have to reschedule. I want to get Lauren settled." He looked
behind him at the antique love seat, but his daughter
wasn't there. He glanced around the large entry that
served as a lobby for the three-story bed-and-breakfast.

He tried to stay calm. "Lauren?"

Mrs. Keenan came around the desk. "I'm sure
she's probably close by, probably just wandered into
the craft shop." The older woman led the way along
a hallway and into a room that housed the usual
touristy things, along with several quilts hanging on
the walls. But there was no sign of his daughter.

Panic rose in his throat. Lauren stayed close by
his side, especially since her mother's death. The
innkeeper walked ahead, then she turned and smiled,
motioning toward an alcove.

Justin froze as he spotted his daughter seated on
a woman's lap. A protective hand rested on Lauren's,
guiding her small fingers through the task of pushing
the needle through the fabric. His chest tightened at
the enchanting scene.

Then other dormant feelings raced through him as

he took in the woman's long auburn hair brushing her shoulders in soft curls and encircling her heart-shaped face. Her pert nose wrinkled when she smiled. She had a fresh-scrubbed look that he found appealing.

"It seems your daughter has found a friend," Mrs. Keenan said, breaking into his thoughts. Then she turned and walked away.

Just then Lauren became aware of his presence. The joy in her eyes faded as she climbed down and hurried to his side.

Justin knelt and wrapped his arms around his daughter. "Lauren, you shouldn't have run off. I was worried."

"Sorry," she whispered.

"Just tell me the next time. Okay?" He rose and turned to the woman who'd managed to gain his daughter's trust. "I'm Justin Hilliard." He held out his hand.

"Morgan Keenan." They shook hands. "And I apologize. I had no idea that Lauren was missing, or that she was your daughter."

"She usually doesn't wander off." Or talk to strangers, he thought.

"Well, she's welcome here anytime." Morgan looked at the child and smiled. "As long as she asks for permission first."

Ms. Keenan was even lovelier close up. Her eyes were a deep emerald-green and expressive. Who would have thought the all-business mayor he'd talked with would turn out to look so soft…so feminine? His throat suddenly went dry. "I don't see it as a problem."

"Good." Morgan brushed her hand against her long skirt. "I hope you and Lauren had a pleasant trip here."

"We had a few delays," he said, his hand on Lauren's shoulder. "I hope my tardiness hasn't caused problems for you."

Morgan shook her head, fighting her nervousness. Justin Hilliard was more handsome than in his magazine and newspaper pictures. Tall, with wide shoulders, he was dressed in jeans, boots and a coffee-colored, cable-knit sweater.

Her attention went to his steel-gray eyes. "I'd planned to spend the day with you… I mean I was scheduled to present the Silver Sky Canyon project."

He frowned. "I apologize. I need to reschedule our meeting." He raised a hand. "It will be at your convenience. Since I've brought Lauren along, I've decided to stay the week. I thought I would mix business with some pleasure time with her."

It was a good sign that a busy CEO like Justin Hilliard was going to be here all week. "That's wonderful. There is so much to see and do around here. I hope you brought some warm clothes. They're predicting snow this week. Probably just flurries, but it's still fun to watch." Why was she babbling? "But then you get snow in Denver." She finally shut her mouth when she saw his smile.

"I'm sorry, Mr. Hilliard. As you can tell I'm anxious to tell you about the project."

"There's no need to apologize and, please, call me Justin."

"And I'm Morgan." She was just happy he was here. She'd been afraid he'd changed his mind. "And yes, we definitely can reschedule our meeting." She glanced at the little girl. "And maybe after you rest Lauren, we can have a look around town."

With questioning eyes, Lauren glanced up at her father.

"I think we both would enjoy a trip around Destiny," he said.

At that moment, Claire Keenan rejoined the group. "Then, let's get you settled Mr. Hilliard. We can send sandwiches up to the suite."

"I don't want to be a bother."

She waved her hand in the air. "Oh, it's not a bother at all. We want you to feel welcome."

Justin looked back at Morgan Keenan. "I thought that was your job."

A delightful blush crossed her cheeks. "I'll do my part, but my mother's cooking is just one of the fringe benefits Destiny has to offer."

The look in his eyes sent a strange feeling coursing through Morgan's veins.

"I can hardly wait to discover the others," he told her.

Morgan walked into the big kitchen, the hub of the Inn and the center of the Keenan family activates. This had been where she and her sisters, Paige and Leah, grew up.

It was the heart of the home, where family problems were discussed and triumphs were cheered, tears shed and laughter shared.

Claire Keenan turned as her daughter entered. "Are they settled in?"

"They seem fine. Thank you, Mom, for handling things."

"It wasn't a problem…we had the suite available."

"I should have booked him there in the first place, but I thought he would fly in only for the day. That he'd fly home tonight." She frowned. "And bringing his daughter with him. That was a surprise."

Her mother smiled. "And she's so sweet. I wonder where her mother is?"

Finding information on Justin Hilliard hadn't been hard. Morgan had gone to her sister. Paige had lived in Denver for nearly ten years and knew all about Hilliard Industries' CEO, both professionally and personally. "He'd been divorced for over a year and has had custody of his daughter since his ex-wife was killed in an automobile accident six months ago."

"How sad," Claire Keenan said. "That poor little thing. So both of them are alone."

Morgan didn't like her mother's curious look. It could only mean trouble. Since Morgan had returned from college, she'd tried to fix her up with every eligible man who'd come to the Inn.

Just then her sisters, Paige and Leah, walked into the kitchen. "Is he here yet?" Leah asked.

Morgan knew who they were talking about. "Yes, he's here," she told them.

"Is he as handsome as his pictures?" Leah asked. The petite blonde couldn't hide the twinkle in her brown eyes as she held out a computer printout from the Hilliard Industries' Web site.

Morgan had to admit that she hadn't expected a hard-driving businessman to be so good-looking. That dark, wavy hair and those gray eyes were… She quickly pushed away the thought.

"His looks have nothing to do with the man building a ski resort here."

Leah frowned. "Now, I am worried. She doesn't even react to a gorgeous man."

"Why are you looking at other men anyway?" Morgan asked. "You two are married women." She glanced pointedly down at their rounded bellies. "And pregnant."

"We're not dead," Paige informed her. The brunette's hair was perfect as was her makeup even though she was eight months pregnant. "Besides, Reed knows I love only him."

"As does Holt," Leah added.

Their mother joined in. "I love your father very much but Justin Hilliard even made me take an appreciative look. And that little girl of his…"

The two sisters turned back to Morgan. "He brought his daughter?" Paige asked.

"That's impressive," Leah added. "How old is she?"

"She's about five and adorable," their mother informed them. "Her name is Lauren and she's already gotten attached to Morgan."

Morgan covered her ears. "Stop it. None if this has anything to do with me getting the man to invest in our town. I haven't even given my presentation."

"You'll ace it," Paige said confidently. "He was interested enough to come here. It's a good invest-ment."

"I still have to convince him."

Morgan wasn't about to tell her family that the man brought it to the surface, causing feelings in her she hadn't felt in a long time. Since college, she'd managed to keep men at arm's length because she wasn't going to chance getting hurt again.

Justin Hilliard could make her change her mind. But for her own sanity, she refused to give that power to a man. Never again.

When they reached the suite, Lauren went right to sleep, which gave Justin time to catch up with cor-respondence from the office. He sat at the antique desk and worked on his laptop, although this wasn't exactly the atmosphere for business. In the corner of the room there was a huge fireplace with a love seat arranged in front of it, along with a plush rug. The bedroom had a huge canopy bed, and the bathroom a large claw-foot tub.

He hadn't originally planned on bringing Lauren along, since the business meeting wasn't supposed to take longer than a day. Lately he made sure he was home in the evenings to be there for his daughter. In the past, he hadn't been much of a part of Lauren's young life, but that was all about to change.

His daughter was going to come first from now on. They were going to be a real family. But first he had to concentrate on business, but he was having trouble.

The memory of Morgan Keenan's pretty face kept popping into his head. And he didn't like that. He'd always prided himself on being able to stay focused on the task at hand.

After pouring a cup of coffee, he went to the window and looked out at the magnificent mountain range encircling the small town of Destiny. The once silver-rich town was thriving no more. Not since the last large mine operation had shut down ten years ago. Now, the few thousand residents remaining had to rely on tourism.

Mayor Morgan Keenan was doing just that, trying to bring industry to her town. Justin was intrigued, both with the town and the woman. Not a good combination, mixing business with pleasure.

Years ago, when his marriage to Crystal failed he decided he was never going to get serious about another woman. He wasn't going to live a celibate life, and when time allowed, he'd been discreet about his female companions, and extra careful not to end up in the tabloids.

He'd had enough of the front page during his circus of a marriage and his ex-wife's many indiscretions. Even after the divorce, Crystal had kept the drama going in his and their daughter's life. But the loss of her mother had been devastating to Lauren.

His child had always been his number one concern. That was what brought him here. They needed to get away from the past, to start a new life…in a new place. Maybe Destiny could be a fresh start for the both of them.

There was a soft knock on the door and Justin went to answer and found Morgan Keenan standing at the threshold.

"I don't want to disturb you or Lauren but we thought you might be hungry." She stepped aside to reveal a cart with sandwiches and milk and coffee.

"Please, come in," he said and moved aside so she could wheel the food tray in.

Morgan placed it in front of the hearth. He watched as the slender woman bent over the table to arrange the meal. Her long skirt prevented him from telling if she had any curves but did catch a glimpse of her slim ankles.

When she started for the door, he blocked her path. "Please, stay and join me," he asked. "I hate to eat alone."

She hesitated, then looked toward the bedroom. "What about Lauren?"

"She's sound asleep." He carried the chair from the desk to the table. "Please, sit."

"You don't have to wait on me."

"A lady should always be seated before a man."

When she passed by him, he caught a whiff of her shampoo. It was some kind of soft, citrus scent. He took a seat opposite her.

"I guess I should have asked if you'd eaten."

She shook her head. "Milk or coffee?"

"Coffee, please." He watched as she poured him a cup, then one for herself. He nodded toward the plate of sandwiches and after she took one, he helped himself to the thin sliced roast beef. It was delicious.

"Would you mind if we went over some questions I have about the project?"

She blinked. "Not at all."

"I'm concerned about access leading to the Silver Sky Canyon. The map shows it's pretty far from the highway."

"That was a problem for a while. The private land owner is my brother-in-law Holt Rawlins. The original road was to cut across his ranch. In fact it's a very beautiful natural area with waterfalls and wonderful hiking trails."

"Sounds like a place I'd like to see."

"It can be arranged for tomorrow, if weather permits." Her gaze locked with his, but she quickly glanced away. "To get back to your question about access to the ski area, we found another way in. It's on the back side of Holt's ranch. It's less intrusive to the environment and there's less chance of disrupting the beauty of the area. Most importantly, Holt is willing to sell the property."

Justin tried to focus on her answers, but found he was more interested in watching her sip her coffee. The slender fingers that held the bone china cup were the same fingers that made the intricate stitches in the quilt downstairs. How would those delicate hands feel on him? He swiftly pushed aside the thought. He was way off track.

"It sounds like you've spent a lot of time working out every detail of this project."

"It's important to me. This town is important to me. I've lived here nearly all my life. And as mayor,

I promised to help bring in revenue. We can't survive without new business resources."

Justin smiled as he got up from the table and went to the window. "The view is breathtaking."

Morgan joined him at the large window overlooking the mountains. "You must have a view of the Rockies in Denver."

"Denver is beautiful, too. But there's something here. A certain peace…serenity that seems to surround the town." He gave her a sideways glance. "I have to say, Morgan, I'm more than intrigued with this area."

Her smile was breathtaking, and so unconsciously seductive that his pulse began to race. She must have felt the change, too.

"I should go." She backed away, but her long skirt caught on the edge of the table and she started to fall. Justin reached for her arm and pulled her upright, but the movement brought her body against his. He immediately responded to her warmth…her softness. Morgan Keenan definitely had curves. But when their gazes met, she began to tremble.

"Are you all right?" he asked.

She nodded, and quickly untangled herself from him. "I'm clumsy sometimes."

"It happens."

"I should help my mother with dinner." Morgan hurried toward the door. "She wanted me to extend an invitation to you and Lauren."

"I don't expect your family to entertain us."

"It's a pleasure. Dinner will be at six," she said,

her hand on the doorknob. "If there's anything you need just call down. Goodbye."

Then she was gone, leaving him to wonder what had happened. Why did she tremble at his touch? There were a great many questions he wanted answered, but the main one was, did he want to get involved with a woman who wouldn't be easy to forget?

He turned back to the scene outside the window. Well, Morgan Keenan would definitely be part of the picture if he decided to make Destiny his permanent home.

"Dinner was delicious, Mrs. Keenan," Justin said as he pushed his plate away with the remains of his second helping of succulent roast pork and potatoes.

"Thank you." She rose from her seat next to her husband at the head of the long table in the Inn's formal dining room. Morgan was seated across from him. She'd changed into a black sweater that accentuated her fair skin. Auburn hair lay in waves around her face. He flashed back to the way she'd felt in his arms.

Not a safe place to go.

He quickly glanced down at Lauren seated beside him. She had wanted to change into a pretty pink dress for tonight, and he done his best to comb her hair and fasten it back with barrettes. Not his best skill.

"I hope you saved room for dessert, Mr. Hilliard," Claire Keenan said. "Morgan made double Dutch apple pie."

"Please, call me Justin."

"And we're Claire and Tim," she said as she collected plates.

Morgan stood and looked at Lauren. "Since you finished all your food, I have a special treat for you." Her smile and emerald gaze moved to Justin. "Of course if it's all right with your father."

The impact was more than he wanted to admit. He turned his attention to his daughter. She'd eaten her food without being coaxed. "Sure."

Morgan held out her hand to the child. "Want to come with me and help?" she asked.

Lauren nodded excitedly as Justin lifted her down and the twosome walked out hand in hand.

"Daughters. They're hard to turn down," Tim Keenan said as the two left.

Justin turned to the big man with the warm smile. He'd caught the loving looks Tim had shared with his wife.

"Lauren's had a rough time. It's hard for me to deny her anything."

"Losing a parent is difficult," Tim agreed. "Our girls lost their biological parents early on. We were truly blessed when they came to us."

Before coming to Destiny, Justin had dug deep into the town's history along with the young mayor's background. He'd learned how close the Keenan family was, and how the town helped raise the girls when they first arrived to town. It was apparent the three sisters had a special bond.

"You must be proud of them."

The older man nodded. "That goes without saying. And it has nothing to do with their careers or what they've chosen in life. Morgan, Paige and Leah turned out to be good people. They're kind and caring, and most importantly, happy. There's nothing more a parent could ask for."

"I'd give anything to make that happen for Lauren."

Tim stared at him. "I'd say you're making a good start. You brought her with you. There's nothing better than spending time with your child."

"It isn't always that simple in my line of work." After seeing her reaction to Morgan and the rest of the Keenan family, he realized how hungry Lauren was for a stable life. He wasn't sure if he could give her that.

Tim leaned back in his chair. "It's only as complicated as you make it. Of course there are choices to make."

"Explain that to my father," Justin said. Marshall Justin Hilliard, Sr. believed in success at all costs. Marriage and family had always come second.

"Hilliard Industries is a large conglomerate, with interests all over the world. I expect it takes a lot of manpower to run, but you should be able to delegate some of the work." Tim arched an eyebrow. "In fact, you could have sent an assistant to oversee this project."

Justin took a drink of his wine, not sure how much he should reveal right now. In the past, honesty had always been his strength in his business dealings and it might be time to lay out his plan.

Morgan came into the room with Lauren. His

daughter was proudly carrying a small dish of ice cream with colorful sprinkles on top. He smiled and helped settle her back in her chair.

There was nothing like seeing Lauren's happiness. "There's a reason I didn't send my assistant."

That drew Morgan's attention from across the table. "It's because if I decide to open a resort here, it won't be a Hilliard Industries investment," Justin began. "It will be mine and Lauren's because...if this project turns out to be right for us, Destiny will also be our home."

CHAPTER TWO

THE next morning in the conference room at City Hall a familiar feeling crept into Morgan's stomach, but she pushed away the nervousness. She could do this. She had worked for years to regain control of her life. She'd earned her position as mayor and the community trusted her to bring in new revenue. She wasn't going to let them down now. She'd gone over her proposal so many times that she could sell the idea to anyone.

But Justin Hilliard wasn't just anyone. Having that good-looking man sitting across the table, studying her closely, was a little intimidating. She'd better get used to it, since he'd announced his plans to live here permanently.

Even without his company behind him, he was powerful in his own right. He could do so much for their small community. Building the resort alone, would mean hiring hundreds of laborers. She felt her own excitement growing and took a calming breath.

"As you can see from the chart, this area is perfect for an extreme ski resort. In fact, the established resorts are booked solid all season and have to turn people away. We're hoping to get the skiers who want a more challenging run."

She pointed to the huge graphics chart that Paige had helped her put together, along with Leah's slide show of the incredible photos she'd taken of the ski area.

"With a new area opening up," she continued, "along with five-star accommodations, we could handle the overflow."

"What about the environmentalists?" Justin asked.

Morgan allowed herself to smile. "We've been okayed for the Silver Sky Canyon area as long as we limit the number of skiers on the mountain. The canyon is perfect for what we have in mind."

"Extreme skiing," Justin said thoughtfully.

She nodded. "It's the big craze right now."

"Won't that drive up the insurance costs?"

Morgan knew she was being tested. Justin Hilliard wouldn't have wasted his time in Destiny if he hadn't checked this all out. She glanced down the table to the town controller/treasurer, Beverly Whiting. The middle-aged woman had been Morgan's biggest supporter since she'd been sworn into office.

"It's all in Beverly's report," Morgan said. "And remember the caliber of skier we'll be catering to. They won't hesitate to pay for the excitement, the adrenaline rush."

Morgan watched as he continued to study the report, then glanced at Paige who smiled encouragingly.

"If I do decide to invest in the resort," Justin Hilliard began, "and build a hotel here, it could cut into some of the businesses in town."

"But if you employ locals in construction it will help our economy immediately, and we'll eventually get revenue from the ski run." In the original deal the town continued to own the land, but they needed an investor to build the resort and run it.

Morgan flipped her chart to the last page to show the mock-up of a planned strip mall next to the hotel complex. "And if you agree, we'd like to add a row of stores available for leasing. No chain fast food places, only fine restaurants, and one-of-a-kind shops."

"Like your quilt shop?"

She shrugged. "We have a silversmith that could make jewelry for shops, and there are artists in the area who would love to sell locally."

"What if I bring in my own people to run things?"

Would he do that? Morgan calmed herself once again. "They will still have to live and shop in Destiny. And I think you know that working with the community is more cost efficient."

Justin Hilliard sat there with his elbows on the table and his fingers steepled together as if thinking of another question. Then he closed his booklet and stood.

"Thank you, Mayor." He shook her hand, then went down to the end of the table and did the same with Beverly and Paige. He came back to Morgan. "Your presentation was impressive."

"This project is close to all of us. Several people

were involved in the planning." She no sooner got the words out when the door opened and Lyle Hutchinson barged into the room.

"Did you think I wouldn't hear about this?" the graying man in his mid-fifties said as he marched up to Morgan. "Just because you're mayor doesn't mean you get to make all the decisions for the town."

This was the last thing Morgan needed today. Lyle Hutchinson, a descendant of one of Destiny's founding families, hated the fact that he didn't have a say-so in this, or a chance for any financial gain from the future ski resort.

"Lyle, you were there when we voted on the project at the last council meeting," Morgan said. "Maybe if you met Mr. Hilliard…"

The usually impeccably groomed banker looked frazzled as he shook a finger in her face. "You aren't going to get away with this. Mark my words I'll stop you if it's the last thing I do."

Justin wasn't going to stand back while this angry man threatened her. He moved around the table.

"I think you better step back from Ms. Keenan," he warned.

The older man glared at Justin. "This isn't your business."

"I'm making it mine." Justin straightened. "For the last time, move away from Ms. Keenan, or I'll move you myself. Your choice."

The man continued to glare at Morgan, but he finally did as Justin suggested. "This isn't over, Morgan. I will remove you from office if it's the last thing I do."

"Please, Lyle," she said. "This isn't the time."

The door opened and a tall man in uniform with a silver badge pinned to his chest came in. He walked right up to the intruder.

"Hutchinson, I don't remember being told you were invited to this meeting." It seemed like old Lyle wasn't popular with anyone.

"If it concerns this town, Sheriff, it concerns me."

"Not if you're disrupting things. You should leave," the sheriff said firmly.

The angry Hutchinson looked as if he was going to argue, but changed his mind. "This isn't the last you hear from me." He turned and stormed out, leaving an uneasy silence in his wake. The sheriff followed him outside.

"I'm so sorry for the disruption," Morgan said.

Justin waved off her apology. "The hell with him. Are you okay?" He studied Morgan's pale face. Although she tried to hide it under oversize clothes, she was delicately built.

"I'm fine, really," she told him. "I can't believe he barged in here like that."

A pregnant Paige Keenan-Larkin came around the table to her sister's side and looked at Justin.

"Mr. Hilliard, Lyle Hutchinson doesn't represent the majority of the citizens who live here. But for many years the Hutchinson family controlled most of what went on in this town." Paige nodded to her sister. "Morgan had the guts to run against him for mayor. Let's just say she sees a new direction for the town. One that didn't profit the Hutchinsons."

The sheriff came back into the room. "I should have known Lyle would show up today. But I just had a little talk with him. I reminded him that he won't get away with intimidation and threats." He looked at Justin. "I'm Reed Larkin, Paige's husband." He stuck out his hand.

"Nice to meet you, Reed. Justin Hilliard." He smiled. "And they say small towns are boring."

Reed grinned. "You just caught us on a good day."

Paige nudged her husband. "Stop it. It's never like this. Mr. Hilliard, Destiny is a quiet town, and most everyone gets along," she assured him. "They elected Morgan because of her ideas on new growth and bringing in revenue."

Justin directed his next question to Morgan. "I take it that Hutchinson is opposed to the ski resort."

She nodded. "He says it will take away from the quaintness of the town, that we'll be overrun with tourists. It's not true. The skiing will be limited, and the resort is five miles out of the town. Besides, the ski lifts will only be open in the winter months."

A hint of a smile appeared on her lovely face. "That's not to say that we're not hoping people return in the summer for hiking, and camping. We have to think about the jobs and the money it will bring into the community." There was passion in her green eyes that had Justin intrigued, not by Morgan as mayor… but as a woman.

Paige Keenan-Larkin spoke up. "As I said, the majority of the citizens like Morgan's fresh new ideas." Paige checked her watch and glanced at her sister. "Morgan, I'm sorry, I have a doctor's appointment but…if you need me to stay."

"No! You go and take care of that niece of mine. She'll be here soon." Morgan hugged her sister. "Reed, you drive her."

"I planned on it." He put his arm around his wife's shoulders and guided her to the door.

Slowly the rest of the people in the room left. Only Justin and Morgan remained. "You have a nice, big family."

"Not that big, but when Paige's and Leah's babies arrive the count will be nine."

Justin envied their closeness. He'd grown up in a large house with servants, but no family to speak of. His father, Marshal Hilliard, had never been home, and his mother wasn't maternal. One day she'd just left, but neglected to take her ten-year-old son with her.

"That's big to those of us who only have two members, just myself and Lauren," he said.

"What about your parents?"

"Let's just say my father has never been much of a family man…and my mother is…has been on an extended vacation."

"I'm so sorry. I don't know what I'd do without my family. It may sound corny but this whole town is like family to me, too. I've lived here most of my life, and wouldn't want to be anywhere else."

"You never wanted to leave?"

"I did once. I went away to college for a few years, but…" A sad look spread across her face. "I missed everyone so much…I decided to come home."

"Did you ever get the chance to finish?"

She nodded. "A few years ago I graduated from Fort Lewis College in Durango."

"That's commendable." He wanted to know more about this woman. "Most people who leave college never go back for their degree."

"My mother wanted me to finish. She didn't exactly nag, but let's say she strongly encouraged me."

Her smile broadened and he found it contagious.

"Always the politician," he said.

"Dad said I was born for this job."

"Well, you certainly have me captivated."

Morgan hated the fact this man could get to her. Justin Hilliard was handsome, powerful and he was flirting with her. But strangely she didn't feel threatened by him.

"Is there anything else?" she asked in an effort to cool down the situation. "I can show you around town before we head out to the resort site."

He checked his watch. "Do we have time to stop by the Realtor's office?"

Morgan's heart rate picked up. "Does that mean you're seriously considering the investment?"

He studied her closely. "If I wasn't serious, I wouldn't be here."

Two hours later, they were headed out to the ranch. Morgan couldn't stop thinking about Justin's words. Was it really possible that this deal would come together?

She turned her car off the road toward the ranch,

then glanced at the man beside her. "The Silver R Ranch has been owned by the Rawlins family for three generations. Holt just recently took over the cattle operation this past year." She smiled. "He's done very well for a New York financial adviser."

"And he's married to your younger sister, Leah."

She gave him a sideways glance. "I take it my mother has been filling you in on the latest news."

He was busy taking in the scenery. "Among other things. She was very kind to offer to watch Lauren today." He drew a breath. "It's beautiful out here. Not a bad backyard."

"I don't think watching your daughter is a hardship." Morgan's gaze went to the vast mountain range she'd taken for granted. The different brown hues of rock blended in with the tall green pines, today all trimmed with a dusting of snow.

"This is nice, but a small town has its downside, too," Morgan said, wanting him to know everything up-front about small-town living. "We have a limited choice of restaurants, no movie theaters close by and everyone knows your business."

"If I do decide to move here and take on this project," he said, "the hotel will have great restaurants, and there's always cable TV. And with a five-year-old, my social life isn't exactly hopping." His face grew serious. "And when you and yours have been splashed all over the media, going out has less appeal. I don't care for myself, but my concern is Lauren. She deserves a chance at a normal life."

Morgan's chest tightened. He was a good dad. If

she could ever consider allowing a man in her life, she could easily fall for this one… A sudden sadness swept over her. She would never be able to have a normal relationship.

No man would want someone with so many emotional scars.

"Morgan…" Justin's voice broke into her thoughts.

"Sorry, I guess I was daydreaming."

"Easy to do here. I feel like I'm playing hooky myself."

"That's how we want everyone to feel when they come to Destiny."

Morgan parked at the back door of the two-story ranch house. It had been recently painted white with dark green trim. The once manicured lawn had the-coming-of-winter golden hue. From the shiny red barn, to the newly strung fencing, Holt had worked hard restoring the place.

"Impressive," Justin said.

"Holt has spent the past year making improvements."

Morgan opened the car door and stepped into the chilly air. She raised her eyes toward the gray sky, and saw threatening clouds overhead. Snow was forecast for later tonight. She hoped it would hold off until they finished the tour. She pulled her coat closer around her body as Justin came to her side. Together they walked up the steps as the back door swung open and Leah appeared.

Her baby sister was petite and cute as could be. Even pregnancy didn't take away from her appeal.

"Welcome," she said as she stepped aside and allowed them inside where it was warm. They passed through a mudroom into a big kitchen with natural wood cabinets and dark granite tops. The original hardwood floors had been refinished and polished to a honey color.

"Leah, this is Justin Hilliard. Justin, my sister Leah."

"It's nice to finally meet you, Mr. Hilliard."

Smiling, Justin took Leah's small hand in his. The Keenan girls were all different and all beauties. The baby sister was blond and adorable. He just happened to prefer the willowy redheaded sister.

"Please call me Justin," he said. "And thank you for letting me have a look around."

"We're excited to have you. I just wish you had a warmer day." Leah turned back to her sister. "I tried to reach you before you left town. There's a slight problem."

"Is it the baby?" Morgan asked anxiously.

"No, the baby's fine. But it's about another baby ready to be delivered. A foal. Shady Lady's in labor and having a rough time. Holt's been with her since early this morning."

Just then the door opened and a young boy rushed in. "Hey, Mom, Dad's going to call the vet. Hi, Aunt Morgan."

The thin blond-haired boy looked about eight or nine. He hugged Morgan.

"Hi, Corey," she said. "How's my favorite nephew?"

He grinned. "I'm fine. I got to help Dad with Lady."

"That's great. Corey, I'd like you to meet Mr. Hilliard. Justin this is my nephew, Corey Rawlins."

"Nice to meet you, sir." Corey nodded and stuck out his hand.

The boy had a firm handshake. "Nice to meet you, too, Corey."

A tall sandy-haired man, dressed in the usual rancher's clothing, jeans, boots and cowboy hat, walked in.

"Man, it's cold out there." He stripped off his sheepskin-lined jacket, hung it on the peg along with his hat and came across the room. "Hi, I'm Holt Rawlins, you must be Justin Hilliard."

"That's me," he said. "I hear from your wife that you're having a little trouble."

Holt went to his wife's side. "Yeah, my prize mare is having a rough time giving birth. I just came up to call the vet and tell Morgan I can't leave right now."

Morgan looked disappointed but hurried to reassure him. "Not a problem, Holt. If you'll loan us the Jeep, we can go on our own."

"Sure." Holt frowned. "Just don't wait too long. There's a storm moving in later this afternoon. I'm sorry, but I've got to call the vet," he said and walked off down the hall.

Justin looked at Morgan. "I guess if we're going, we better leave soon."

"Sure," Morgan said, and turned to her sister. "Sorry to run off."

"I'd go with you," Leah began as she rubbed her slightly rounded stomach, "but I don't think baby would appreciate a lot of jostling around." She picked a nylon basket up off the counter. "At least I can send something with you. It's just coffee and some snacks."

Justin took the basket. "Thank you, Leah, that was thoughtful." He raised an eyebrow. "We better get going, Morgan."

"Thanks, Leah."

"I just want to help with the project." She smiled at Justin. "You're going to fall in love with the site."

Holt returned and slipped on his coat. "Vet's on his way. I'll walk you down to the barn."

There was a long, lingering kiss between Leah and Holt that anyone who didn't have a special someone in their life would envy. Justin glanced at Morgan. Was there someone special for her?

"You ready?" Holt asked breaking into Justin's thoughts.

With a nod, he followed Morgan to the door and the three of them walked to the barn where an old Jeep was parked. With a wave, Holt hurried off to the barn.

"I guess we're on our own," Justin said.

"It's not a problem," Morgan said. "I've been up to this area a hundred times."

Morgan wasn't concerned about the drive as much as the weather. Snow was predicted. If Justin Hilliard didn't see the site today, he might lose interest. At the very least, it would slow the project that she hoped would start in the early spring.

"We better hurry since snow is predicted for later tonight. This looks like our window of opportunity."

Justin walked around to the passenger's side of

the Jeep. "Then let's do it now. I like seeing what I'm buying."

His words sent a fresh ripple of excitement through her. She was going to make this happen, even if it meant spending considerable time alone with a man. Something she'd avoided for a long time.

The ride was bumpy, but going up this side of the mountain was the best way to see the future ski run. Morgan hoped that Justin felt the same way she did when he saw Silver Sky Canyon.

She parked the Jeep along the crest of the canyon opposite the ranch. "Come on, I want to show you the ultimate selling point." She opened the door, climbed out and Justin followed.

She carefully made her way to the ledge. Ignoring the wind whipping her hair, she took out her stocking cap and covered her head as she peered down at the canyon. There was little snow to hide the incredible rock formations along with the huge pines lining either side of the natural slope. At the base, the land flattened out.

"You were right this view is unbelievable," Justin said. "One would almost hate to do anything to change it."

"We actually aren't going to have to change much," she began. "Remember this isn't going to have a bunny hill, the slope is too steep. This canyon is perfect for the *extreme* skier."

He continued to study the area. "I did research on

this new phenomenon, and it's catching on, big time."

"And just think of all the ski gear they wear. The pro shop in the hotel could do big business just on equipment alone. Also there would be a ski pro and tour guides… Anyone using this slope will have to complete a specific number of ski classes."

Justin watched the beginning of snow flurries dance around Morgan's face. It was hard to stay on task when he was being distracted by this woman. It was a good thing that he'd done most of his research before coming here.

"And you probably have locals to fill those jobs, too."

She nodded. "Why not hire the best? The ones who know the area, who have skied these mountains since they were kids."

She was good. "Is there access from the highway?" He moved closer to her as she pointed down to a road.

"This is the back side of Holt's ranch. He's willing to sell us the land needed to get to the ski area."

"How far is it from the highway?"

"Ten miles." She motioned to the area. "It's scenic all the way in. And the only stipulation Holt asked for is no large billboards to mar the countryside."

Morgan glanced at him and their gazes locked momentarily, but it was enough to send a surge of awareness through him. He swallowed the dryness in his throat. "I agree with Holt on that. I'm liking this idea more and more."

She smiled and stepped back, suddenly losing her balance. He grabbed her hand and pulled her upright.

"Be careful," he said, not releasing her. Instead he walked her away from the ledge. "Maybe we should talk back here."

Morgan pulled her hand away. "I lie, I am this clumsy." Suddenly there was a strong wind mixed with snow.

He glanced up at the sky. "Maybe we shouldn't stay any longer. The storm is coming in sooner than expected."

Morgan agreed, a little angry with her reaction to Justin. They walked back to the Jeep and got in. She started the engine, hoping that she could make it back to the ranch without any more mishaps. But when she peered out the windshield at the white haze, she knew it wasn't going to be easy.

She turned on the wipers. "Well, here comes the snow that was forecast."

Slowly she backed up on the crest, maneuvered the vehicle around and started down the steep grade.

"This has really picked up," Justin said as he stared out. "Are you all right driving?"

"I'm okay." She hit a rut and gripped the wheel tighter. She wasn't sure if she was shivering from the cold, or from nervousness. "I'm just taking it slow, because visibility is so bad."

"If you want I'll drive," he offered.

She didn't dare take her eyes off the road. "Really, I'm doing fine," she lied. Had she been crazy to bring him up here today? Would he think she was? At this point she didn't care. The Jeep went over a big rock and bounced hard. She knew the trail pretty well, but she'd never had to tackle it during a snowstorm.

"This is like an amusement park ride," he tried to joke.

"Can I get off?" she kidded back.

"I'm with you on that."

Just then the Jeep hit another rut, and this time went sideways. She turned the wheel back, but not in time to stop the Jeep from heading toward a group of rocks. There was a horrible scraping sound from underneath the vehicle and suddenly they jerked to a stop. She gasped as she was thrown forward. The old Jeep's seat belts were useless, and she bumped the windshield.

"Are you all right?" Justin asked, reaching for her.

She nodded. "What happened?" She glanced out to see the Jeep sitting at an angle.

"We went off the path. Sit tight, I'll go check," he said, grabbed the flashlight from the glove compartment and climbed out into the blinding snow.

It seemed to take forever but he finally returned to the cab. She could barely see what he was doing, and worried that he could fall and hurt himself. God. What a mess. What a mistake she'd made.

The door opened and a blast of cold air hit her as he climbed into the seat, snow covering his coat. "The boulder tore out the transfer case."

Morgan had no idea what that was. "Is it important?" That sounded so dumb. "Of course it's important."

"It is, if you want the Jeep to move forward, or in reverse. Besides, we'll need help to get off the rock."

"So we're stuck here." This wasn't good.

"We should call Holt. Is there any reception here?"

Lord, she hoped so. She took out her cell phone and saw the bars were nearly nonexistent. "Sometimes yes, and sometimes no." She punched in the ranch house.

"Hello," Leah answered. "Morgan, where are you?"

"It's a long story. We're stuck about halfway down the mountain. The Jeep is…disabled. Do you think Holt could come get us?"

Her brother-in-law came on the phone. "Morgan, I'll try but in this weather, it may take a while. Just in case, you need to take cover."

Morgan looked around. The snow blanketed everything, but she'd been on outings with her dad. He'd taught all his daughters how to survive in the mountains. Did she remember anything? "Can't we stay in the Jeep?"

"Not if the snow keeps up. Look, I'll call Reed and we'll try to get through the pass before it's blocked. You need to give me some landmarks."

She looked at Justin. "Holt needs landmarks."

Without hesitation, Justin stepped out of the cab and looked into the dim late-afternoon light. When he returned, he took the phone from her.

"Holt, we're about two miles down from the summit and there's a huge rock formation that looks like a church steeple." He paused and listened, then reached in his pocket and wrote something down. "Yes. Yes, I'll try to call you when we reach it. Thanks." He pocketed her phone. "Bundle up. We have a short hike to a cave. Holt said it's the one Corey stayed in."

"I know that place." It still didn't ease her fears.

His eyes met hers. "Then we need to get going." He grabbed the basket from the back and a blanket and flashlight off the rear seat. "Holt said the cave was about a quarter of a mile from here." He rummaged through the glove compartment, took out a lighter and stuffed it in his pocket. "We can wait out the storm there."

Morgan buttoned her coat and tugged on her gloves. She released a breath, oddly feeling a calm take over. With a nod, she took the blanket, opened her door and followed Justin down the mountain trail.

For the first time in a long time she was about to trust a man she barely knew.

CHAPTER THREE

LOSING daylight and with the wind against them, it wasn't easy to get to their destination. Justin was shielding her as much as he could from the bone-chilling cold. Finally they reached the familiar ledge and he gave her a boost onto the rock, handed her the basket, then he braced his arms and jumped up.

Gathering their things, Justin shone the flashlight onto the ground as they continued to search for the elusive cave opening…and warmth.

"It's around here somewhere," Morgan called out as Justin illuminated the side of the mountain. He stayed close to her as they walked among the rocks.

"Here," she called. "It's here." She picked up the pace and headed to the opening.

She allowed him to go first. He had to duck his head at the entrance, but once inside there was room to stand up in the dark cave.

"Stay here." He set down the basket, and began walking around, shining the flashlight along the walls.

Morgan could see that other humans had taken

shelter here. There was a rough log, and next to it a pit that once held a fire. "Good, it seems to have enough ventilation to warm up the place." He turned to her. "Best part we don't seem to have to share it with any animals."

Shivering, Morgan hugged herself. "So we'll be safe here?"

"A lot better than out there. But I better get some firewood before it gets too dark." He walked to the opening.

She started to follow him.

"You stay here where it's warmer."

"Why? I can gather wood," she said.

"Okay, but stay close." His expression was clouded in the dim light as he pulled out the cell phone and called Holt. The reception kept breaking up, but he was able to tell him that they'd made it safely to the cave.

"At least Leah won't worry," Morgan said.

"Holt can't risk coming out tonight. I'm glad your mother is staying with Lauren."

"I am grateful for that."

They didn't have to go far because there was a downed tree about twenty feet from the cave. Morgan gathered twigs while Justin broke off the bigger branches. Finally loaded down, they lugged their bounty back to the cave. All the time, she couldn't stop blaming herself for this mess, especially for him having to spend the night away from his daughter…

Plus, she would be spending it with a man who was practically a stranger.

With the aid of the flashlight, Justin placed the twigs and some pine needles in the fire ring and pulled a lighter from his pocket.

"Remind me to thank Holt for keeping this in the Jeep." He flicked the lighter and touched the flame to the combustible material. After a few seconds, it took off. He quickly added more twigs, until the fire was blazing, illumining their temporary quarters.

He sat down on the log. "Not bad for a city guy, huh?"

"It's nice and warm." She spread her hands closer to the flames. "A lot better than being out there." The wind whistled past the entrance. "I can't tell you how sorry I am that this happened."

He shrugged. "You can't take the blame for the weather." He turned to her with his silver-gray gaze.

She looked away. "How am I going to tell Holt that I tore out the underside of his Jeep?"

"I don't think that matters to him as much as your safety."

"He warned us about the storm."

"And if I hadn't delayed us by stopping by the Realtor's office, we would have gotten an earlier start. But let's stop with the what-if's. I'm just grateful that we're both safe."

Morgan looked away, but she couldn't help being drawn to his seductive voice, or his mesmerizing gaze. It had been a long time since a man had made her feel this way.

She felt his hand on her arm and jumped.

"Sorry, I didn't mean to startle you," he apologized, but he looked confused.

"I guess I'm still a little nervous."

He gave her a half smile. "I'd say this trip has been a little...adventurous."

"Adventurous?" She found herself laughing out loud.

Justin joined in. "You have a nice laugh," he said as he studied her. "And a pretty smile."

"Thank you." Not knowing how to deal with the compliment, Morgan busied herself by opening the nylon basket and pulling out the thermos. "Oh, good, Leah sent us some nourishment." She took off the lid and inhaled the rich coffee aroma. "This should help keep us warm."

Morgan handed him a cup, then searched through the basket, found another and filled it for herself.

As Justin held the warm plastic cup between his hands, he couldn't help but watch Morgan Keenan. She was easy to look at, maybe too easy. He was pleasantly surprised when she'd showed up today in jeans. They emphasized what he'd already suspected: long slender legs and a shapely bottom.

Everything about Morgan Keenan intrigued him. She was smart and brave. And made no complaints about her discomfort. Crystal would have been screaming her head off, demanding he took her back...

"Are you hungry?" she asked, breaking into his thoughts. "Leah packed sandwiches." She examined one. "Ham and cheese or turkey."

He put another log on the fire and brushed his hands

on his jeans as he glanced into the basket. "By the looks of things, she was expecting us to stop for a picnic."

"I for one am glad she did."

He nodded. "I'll take the ham and cheese, unless you want it."

She handed it to him. "No, I prefer turkey."

Justin opened the bag, pulled out one half of the sandwich and took a big bite. It was the best ham and cheese ever.

"Have you ever gotten stranded up here before?" he asked.

She shook her head. "It's been a while since I've been one-on-one with nature. I mean, I believe we need to protect the environment and all, but I haven't had much time for hiking and camping outdoors. I'm the bookworm of the family." She smiled nervously, knowing she was rambling. "Now Leah, she'd think this was a wonderful adventure. She's been traipsing around these mountains photographing everything since high school. That's how she met Holt. He caught her trespassing. And believe me, back then he wasn't too happy to find her on his land." She had to stop her chattering.

"That's hard to believe. The guy's crazy about her."

Morgan looked at him. "He is now."

He studied her for a moment. "I have no doubt that all the Keenan girls could be very convincing."

She didn't want this to turn personal. It was distracting enough being in a cave with the good-looking man.

"Did I tell you that my nephew, Corey, hid out in this cave for a while?" They had a long night ahead of them…together.

"He's just a kid."

"He was a runaway back then. That's how Leah and Reed connected. They teamed up and went out and searched for him. The boy ran away from a bad foster home, and Holt took him in."

Justin took another bite. "And now they all live happily ever after."

"It happens sometimes." Morgan concentrated on her sandwich. "What about you, Justin? You seemed pretty good at gathering wood and starting a fire."

"I did do a few years in the Boy Scouts. I liked camping and hiking, but my dad was too busy to come along. I got tired of making excuses for him not showing up and just dropped out." He stole a glance at Morgan and saw the compassion in her eyes.

"I'm sorry," she said.

Justin shrugged as if it hadn't bothered him, but Marshal Hilliard not having time for his only son had hurt. "It's not a big deal."

"It is a big deal," Morgan argued. "Parents should spend time with their kids." Suddenly she looked mortified. "I had no right to say that. No doubt your father was a busy man."

"Please, don't apologize. Marshal Hilliard was a driven man, but not by his family. By business." Justin finished his sandwich and put the empty wrapper in the basket. "I don't want that for Lauren.

That's the reason I'm considering buying into this project—to get away from the big corporate life."

"Being CEO of a major company is a big responsibility."

"It can consume your life, too." He thought back to his failed marriage. "I also have no privacy and everything I do is scrutinized. That's hard when you want a personal life, and have a child."

"Lauren is precious. I can see why you're so protective."

The glow of the fire illuminated Morgan's pretty face. She had removed her cap, and her auburn hair was lying in soft curls around her shoulders. It had been a long time since a woman distracted him.

"My daughter is the most important person in my life. She's had entirely too much pain in her short life." He stared down at the fire. "First the divorce, then there was her mother dying in the accident." He paused. "Lauren was in the car, too." He heard Morgan's gasp, but continued. "I blame myself for many of the problems in my marriage. For a long time I wasn't there for Crystal…or Lauren. It was only after she died that I learnt the true extent of my wife's alcohol and drug abuse."

"I'm sorry, Justin."

Tonight, Justin didn't want to be thinking about his past mistakes. "I don't want pity."

"It's not pity, but I am sad that you and your child had to go through all the pain. You didn't cause your wife's addictions. She did that on her own."

"Then why do I feel so guilty?"

"Because when someone you love lets you down, it hurts, and it's easy to think it was your fault."

Justin studied her, seeing the flash of pain in her eyes. "You sound like you've experienced it, too."

She glanced away. "It was a long time ago." She busied herself, looking into the basket, and pulled out a bag of cookies. "Want one?"

"Sure." He took the homemade peanut butter cookie. "Was this guy the reason you quit college?"

Her eyes widened. "That was part of it."

Morgan stood, pulled her coat together and walked to the entrance. She hoped Justin would figure out that she didn't want to talk about this. He didn't, feeling him coming up behind her.

"Did someone hurt you, Morgan?"

"We all get hurt." She closed her eyes, fighting off the dark memories. Even after all this time, the pain was still there. Her heart began to pound, her breathing quickened. She leaned outside to gather more oxygen into her tight chest.

"Was he your boyfriend?" Justin stayed close, his voice soothing and nonthreatening, but she couldn't share the dark time in her life. She never had and never would.

"It was so long ago..."

"We all remember our first experience of being in love."

If only she could forget. If only she could block out that awful night.... She drew a steady breath. "Maybe we should talk about something else."

When she started to walk away, he reached for her. She panicked and jerked away. "Don't touch me."

Justin immediately raised his arms in surrender. "It was never my intension to offend you. I just wanted to say that I'm sorry you were hurt."

She brushed her hair back. "No, I overreacted. It's being in this situation, being here."

"We're okay, we'll be out in the morning." He frowned. "But if I'm making you nervous, or uncomfortable, I apologize. I also assure you that you have nothing to worry about."

He walked away and sat down on the log.

"Justin, it's not you." She released a sigh when he turned to face her. "This is a crazy situation for both of us. And this project is so important to me that—"

"You're going to fight the attraction between us," he finished for her. "And you're wondering if it will mess up the business deal?"

She couldn't say anything to that.

"Well, let me assure you that I want the Silver Sky Ski Run as much as you do. But I have to be honest with you, Morgan. The minute I set eyes on you holding my daughter on your lap, I felt something." He paused. "I think you feel it, too."

Morgan didn't know what to say. She was afraid he would walk away, and she wasn't so sure it was only the business part she cared about. And that scared her to death.

"It wouldn't be a good idea," she told him. "Not if we're going to work together."

He took a step closer. "Don't you think I know that? I want this deal to go through, too. From everything I've learned about the town of Destiny, it sounds like a perfect place to raise my child, and start a new life. The last thing I expected to think about was getting involved. Then you appeared…"

Morgan was thrilled by his words, but at the same time terrified. "This is crazy. You've only been here two days. It's just the extraordinary circumstances…"

"That, too. But whenever I'm around you, there's this awareness between us. Yet, I feel that makes you nervous." His eyes were so kind and understanding. "I never want you to be afraid of me. And you are…"

She couldn't deny it.

"Morgan, just tell me is it me, or is it all men?"

Morgan had no intention of getting this personal with a virtual stranger. A man she'd barely known for forty-eight hours. Most important, he was a possible business partner.

"Look, Justin." She drew a breath. "If a relationship is connected with the finalizing of this deal, then you can turn around and go back to Denver." She held her breath, studying his clenched jaw, knowing she could have just blown this project.

"I apologize if I've made you feel uncomfortable. It was never my intention." His gray-eyed gaze locked with hers. "I won't lie to you, Morgan, there is an attraction, but I'd never use you to get the Silver Sky project."

Morgan didn't know if her shivering had to do with Justin's admission, or from the cold. She didn't want to think about it, either, or the fact that she'd felt the same pull he did. But there was no way there could ever be anything between them.

She wouldn't trust him or any man again.

"This is a business proposition." She paused. "It's the only way, Justin." Her own words didn't help her empty feeling, or the constant, lonely ache around her heart. For just an instant she thought about taking a chance. But she knew she wouldn't. Couldn't.

Justin could see the pain in Morgan's green eyes. He wanted nothing more than to take her in his arms and reassure her he would never hurt her, or let anyone hurt her again.

"Who hurt you, Morgan? Who was the man who stole your trust?"

She looked shocked, and then closed up completely. "I'm not going to discuss my private life with you." She moved past him and went back to sit on the log.

Justin couldn't let it go. "You're right. I have no business asking you personal questions." He hesitated, not taking his own advice. "But I've been there, Morgan. You can't keep running away... believe me I've tried."

Her head snapped up and her eyes narrowed. "You don't know enough about me to make assumptions."

"I think you've been hurt...badly. And you haven't let it go." He straddled the log, far enough away not to threaten her.

She tried to laugh, but it caught in her throat. "It has nothing to do with you." She blinked rapidly. "Our connection is business. Please remember that."

She was breaking his heart. "If I decide to take on this project, Morgan, I'll be around. We'll be working together. It's a little awkward if every time I get near you, you jump."

"I don't normally," she denied. "But you have to admit that these circumstances are a little unsettling." There was a hint of a smile as she hugged herself. "I've never conducted business dealings in a cave."

"I think this is a first for me, too," he said as he added another branch to the fire. The temperature had dropped, and the wind was still howling just outside.

"Why don't we set aside all business until tomorrow?" He stole another glance at her. "Maybe you could tell me about growing up in Destiny."

She smiled. "You might get a prejudiced account. I love this town. From the moment I arrived, I knew I didn't want to live anywhere else."

He frowned. "You weren't born here?"

She shook her head. "No, but I was only three, and my sisters were even younger, when we were left in the Keenans's care. Our mother said she was coming back but she never did. Circumstances beyond her control made that impossible. It was about a year later that the Keenans adopted us. So Destiny is really the only home we've had."

Justin watched as emotions played across her pretty face.

She came out of her daze. "I'm sorry," she breathed. "It's a pretty boring story."

Nothing about this woman could bore him. "It must have been nice to know most everyone in town."

"It was. The entire town sort of pulled together to help Mom and Dad raise us." She smiled again. "They even nicknamed us Destiny's Daughters."

"I bet Lyle Hutchinson wasn't so nice."

"That's not true. Both Lyle and his father, Billy Hutchinson, were very active in the goings-on in town. It's just that a lot has happened lately to the founding family that's threatened their status in Destiny. Billy's now in a nursing home with Alzheimer's, Lyle is having trouble with his father's illness and the progress in town."

"And you're all for progress."

She grew serious. "It's not like when the mines were open, and employing hundreds of workers. The town needs new revenue."

Justin liked to listen to her. She cared about the town and its people. That was what he liked the most about Destiny and its mayor. "That's where I come in."

"Hopefully. It's a very good investment, or you wouldn't be here."

"Whether it is or isn't, Lauren is my main focus." His gaze held hers. "She deserves to have a normal childhood. I don't want a housekeeper or nanny to raise her. I want to be there to pick her up from school. To help her with homework, share her meals."

"It's hard being a single parent, Justin," Morgan said. "But everyone needs help."

"Would you help, Morgan?"

She finally looked at him. "Help you with what?"

"I want Lauren to have a childhood like you and your sisters had. And that's the reason I've decided to take on the Silver Sky project."

CHAPTER FOUR

MORGAN shivered from the cold and burrowed closer to the source of heat. Slowly a soothing band of strength wrapped around her, drawing her in. She purred at the complete feeling of solace as she inhaled the earthy male scent that was so intoxicating.

All at once she realized a different feeling as a hand moved over her back in a circular motion. It wasn't long before her breathing changed and tightness erupted in her stomach as she tried to absorb the new feelings. Then she felt the touch, a soft caress against her cheek, which sent shivers down her spine. She tipped her head back, wanting...

"Morgan..."

Morgan heard her name through her sleepy fog, but the erotic feeling kept pulling her back. The pleasure was too great...too intense for her to want it to end.

"Morgan...wake up," the man's voice whispered.

The familiar voice jarred her and she blinked to find Justin Hilliard staring at her. Suddenly she realized that she was practically lying on top of him.

She jumped back. "Oh, my. I'm sorry."

He sat up, too. "It's okay, Morgan."

"It's not okay," she argued. She tried to move away, but she was lodged in between the log and him.

"We were only trying to stay warm." He had the nerve to smile. "And I didn't mind helping out."

She gasped, looking at his large chest, covered by soft flannel. "Was I like that…with you…all night."

Justin ran a hand through his hair. "No, just the last hour or so. The fire probably died out. We needed body heat for warmth."

"You should have woken me up."

His mouth twitched in amusement. "Having a beautiful woman in my arms wasn't exactly an unpleasant experience for me."

Morgan felt a sudden rush of heat through her body, realizing this had been the first man she'd let get this close in a long time. And it was wrong. They were going to be business associates.

She started to argue that point when she heard, "Morgan! Justin! Hey, help has arrived."

They both looked toward the entrance and saw Holt and Reed standing there.

"Seems you two managed to stay warm," Reed said.

Morgan climbed to her feet. "Holt! Reed! Are we happy to see you."

"Yes," Justin said as he got up, too. "We ran out of Leah's peanut butter cookies."

"She'll be so glad you're both all right that I'm sure she'll make you another batch."

Morgan drew Holt's attention. "Holt, I'm sorry about the Jeep. I'll pay for any damage."

"No, I'll pay," Justin said. "It was my fault we started so late."

"I should have known better," Morgan countered. "So it's my fault."

Justin turned to the two men. "Are all the Keenan women so stubborn?"

Holt and Reed exchanged a glance, then Holt said, "Only if they think they're right."

"It just so happens I am about this. I pay." Morgan gathered up their things. "Come on, I want to get out of here."

She needed to put some space between herself and Justin. That was the only way this project was going to work.

The trip down the mountain was easy, since the snow had nearly melted away by the sun. When they arrived at the ranch, Morgan saw that the entire family was waiting for them. Justin climbed out of the sheriff's four-wheel drive vehicle and hurried up on the porch to little Lauren.

"Daddy! Daddy!" she cried as she raised her arms for him to lift her up. He did, and swung her around in a circle as he kissed her cheeks.

All Morgan could do was stand back and watch. Watch as Leah hugged Holt, Paige reached for Reed, even her parents had each other.

She was the odd one out.

Her parents rushed to her and they exchanged hugs. "Oh, Morgan, we were so worried."

"Well, we were fine. We found shelter and built a fire." They'd always been there for her and she loved them for that.

The group stepped into the warm kitchen where Leah had breakfast nearly ready.

"Daddy, I helped Mrs. K. and Leah to make breakfast for you."

Corey ran up to Morgan. "I'm glad you're okay, Aunt Morgan."

"So am I." She hugged him. "And thanks to you for finding that cave. It sure came in handy last night."

"Did you build a fire?"

Justin set his daughter down. "Yes, thanks to the lighter I found in the Jeep."

Holt grinned. "Glad I could help. If you want to clean up before breakfast, there's a shower upstairs."

"Daddy, we packed some clothes for you," Lauren said. "I helped a lot."

"I bet you did." He turned to Claire. "I can't thank you enough for watching her."

The older woman smiled. "You're welcome. She was a joy to have around." She looked at Morgan. "I brought you some clean clothes, too."

Before Morgan could say she'd wait until she got home, her sister nudged her up toward the stairs.

"Use our bathroom," Leah insisted, then turned to Justin. "Justin, your bag is in the guest bedroom at the top of the steps, and the bathroom is right across from it." Then she sent them off each with a mug of coffee, telling them breakfast would be served in twenty minutes.

Morgan rushed on ahead, not wanting to be coupled with Justin any longer. Not this man who'd made her feel things…things she thought she'd never feel again.

Standing in the shower she let the warm water wash over her, but it did nothing to relieve the tension from her night with Justin, or the memory of waking up in his arms this morning.

After putting on clean underwear, a pair of jeans and a warm peach-colored sweater, Morgan pulled her hair up with a rubber band and headed back to the kitchen. She came down the hall toward the stairs when the bath room door opened and she collided with Justin. Her hands went to his bare chest as he grabbed her to steady her. That was when she realized that, except for a towel around his waist, he was naked. Her heart rate suddenly went crazy as his gaze leveled on her, then an apologetic smile appeared on his freshly shaven face.

"I'm sorry…I left my clothes in the bedroom," he told her.

"Well…then, I should let you get dressed." She pulled back, but couldn't help admiring his broad chest and trim waist. Thoughts of sleeping against his strength flooded her head and her entire body reacted with a jolt.

Her gaze went to his face. "They're probably holding breakfast for us."

"Probably." He didn't move. "Morgan, about last

night… Please believe what I said, I'd never take advantage of the situation. You have my word."

Justin wasn't the guilty party. She was. "I know. I'm the one who should apologize to you. I was the one stealing your warmth."

He smiled. "I think it's safe to say we had plenty of heat to keep each other warm."

Oh, boy, did he ever. "It was only out of necessity."

"Of course, necessity." He shook his head. "It's been an interesting forty-eight hours. I can't wait to see what's next."

Surprisingly Morgan was curious about the same thing. It both thrilled and frightened her.

Every chance he got, Justin stole a glance at Morgan across the kitchen table. They'd all finished a hearty breakfast, then sat back to enjoy another cup of coffee.

Nine-year-old Corey had taken Lauren into the den to watch a video with a promise to visit the new foal later.

"So where are you planning to live?" Holt asked.

Justin jerked his attention back to the conversation. "I'm not sure. Probably in town, and I'll commute to the site when we begin construction. I do want to be settled in a home right away. I don't want to be going back and forth to Denver. It's not good for Lauren."

Claire Keenan refilled the coffee mugs. "She was so worried last night when you didn't come home. I reassured her that you were safe from the cold in a cave with Morgan."

"What did she say to that?"

The older woman smiled. "She turned the tables on me and began reassuring me that her daddy would take care of Morgan. In Lauren's words. 'If Morgan gets scared Daddy can hold her real tight until all the monsters go away.'"

Every eye turned to Justin and he felt uncomfortable.

"That's so sweet," Leah said, then sent a questioning look to Morgan. "Were you scared?"

Morgan's gaze jerked to Justin's, then quickly looked away before he could read her thoughts. She turned to Leah. "Only when I hit the rock and tore out the underside of the Jeep."

Laughter filled the kitchen, along with a feeling of family that Justin had never experienced before. He glanced around the table to see love expressed in every look, every touch…in every word. This was something he'd been searching for his entire life.

"Have you talked with a real estate agent?" Morgan asked.

He nodded. "I'm scheduled to look at a home later today. The big colonial on Birch Street."

"The old Calloway place?"

"Yes. Is there a problem?" Justin asked.

"Only it's going to take time, and a lot of money to restore," Tim told him. "The place hasn't been lived in for years."

"That's Morgan's house," Paige jumped in. "The one she always wanted to live in. Remember?"

Justin caught Morgan's blush. "Your house?"

"I was ten years old when I said that," she replied glaring at her sister. "It's a great house, but Lyle Hutchinson owns it."

"Oh, the rude man I told to leave your office?"

"Don't worry, when it comes to money, Hutchinson doesn't hold a grudge," Morgan assured him.

"I hope so," Justin said. "I'd like the chance of restoring the place back to the original state."

"It's pretty run-down," Claire said. "It was once owned by a wealthy miner. After he went broke, he had to sell it." Her smile brightened. "Oh, it's nice that it's going to be a family home again. You should ask Morgan for help with the decorating. She's our history buff."

Destiny's mayor continued to amaze him. "Maybe you'd be willing to give me some pointers on things."

Morgan groaned inwardly. She didn't need to spend any more time with Justin Hilliard. "Aren't you getting ahead of yourself? Lyle hasn't even agreed to sell."

"I'm pretty good at convincing when I want to be."

Her breath grew rapid. "Maybe…you won't like the house once you've seen the inside."

"The structure looks solid, although the porch columns will probably have to be replaced, and I can't imagine not loving the architecture inside." His gaze met Morgan's. "I could use your help."

Morgan should be excited about all this, but there were her usual doubts…and fears. She knew how important it was to work with this man. She'd already agreed to that. So what would it hurt to look at the house? Nothing, as long as she remembered she was doing this for the town…and the citizens who'd always been there for her and her sisters.

"Why don't we finalize the ski lodge deal with the city council, then we can discuss it," Justin said.

"I don't foresee anything that we can't compromise on." Morgan was sure, too. She'd like to add that she could only see Justin during business hours. But she knew with him living at the Inn, they'd run into each other.

He made her feel needy and vulnerable and she didn't like that at all. Oh, yes, she needed to avoid Justin Hilliard at all costs.

Justin Hilliard had returned to Denver two days ago. Morgan hated to admit it, but she'd missed both the man…and his daughter. She'd kept busy finishing the proposal for the council meeting, but she'd still managed to reminisce about their time together.

It had been so long since she let a man interest her. Nearly ten years. Not since college…and Ryan.

She'd been so young, and eager to go away to school. Wide-eyed and naive, she'd fallen in love with the idea of being on her own. And in one short year, her idyllic life had been destroyed. Her innocence lost.

Worse, because of a man, she'd lost what was most important—herself.

"Mayor Keenan," George Pollen called to her.

She shook away the thoughts. "Excuse me, what did you ask?"

The owner of the Gold Mine Steak House pointed to the financial sheet. "You said that Mr. Hilliard has read over and signed the contract."

"Yes, he has." She held up the papers. "He overnighted the contracts to me and I received them this morning."

She'd remembered back to their lengthy phone conversation. It hadn't been all about business. Justin asked about other things, like family and their lives... He even talked about Lauren and his daughter's excitement about coming to live in Destiny.

Morgan felt that same excitement.

She glanced around the eight-person council. "Now, all that is left to do is vote on awarding the Silver Sky Canyon project to Justin Hilliard."

She eyed the panel again for any protest.

"When I call your name, please say yea, or nay." She began reading off names, knowing pretty much who would and wouldn't agree to this project. When she reached Lyle Hutchinson, she didn't even pause when he called out, nay.

After the roll call it was five to three in favor of the project. Hers was the deciding vote to get the two-thirds needed to pass.

"And I vote, yea. The majority has it. Justin Hilliard wins the bid to start the project in the spring." She raised her gavel and hit the block. "This meeting is adjourned."

Applause broke out as Lyle Hutchinson glared at her. "I hope you're not sorry for this," he said as he marched out the door.

Morgan hoped so, too.

"Daddy, is Morgan waiting for us at the Inn?" Lauren asked.

"I don't know, sweetie." Justin glanced around at his daughter strapped securely in the back seat of his SUV. "She might be at work."

"She said I could help her make her quilt when I came back."

"Well, Morgan might be busy." He hoped she could find some time to spend with him. That it wouldn't be only to discuss business.

"I know, Daddy. She is the boss of the whole town."

He bit back a grin. "She does have an important job."

"Corey says Aunt Morgan has to tell everybody what to do. Will she be the boss of you, too?"

Justin glanced in the rearview mirror and saw those big blue eyes that had stolen his heart over and over again since the day she was born.

"Let's just say, we'll be working together. And Morgan isn't the boss of the town. She just makes sure everything runs smoothly."

"Oh." Lauren's attention went to the window as they approached the outskirts of Destiny. "Can we go see our new house?"

"Our house isn't exactly new, sweetie. Remember I told you that it needs some work before we move in."

A dozen times in the past seventy-two hours, he'd wondered if he'd done the right thing packing up and moving them both to a new town, away from everything that was familiar to Lauren.

Justin wasn't happy that he'd left Denver without resolving things with his father. Of course it hadn't been the first time that Marshall Hilliard was disappointed in his son. In two years Justin would turn thirty-five. At that point he was supposed to take over the CEO position at Hilliard Industries. It had been something his father wanted, never him.

Not to say he hadn't tried his father's way, but now, after a failed marriage, and with a daughter to raise, he had to decide what was important. What he wanted out of life.

"I'm glad we're staying at the Inn," Lauren said, breaking into his thoughts.

"So you like it here in Destiny?"

Her head bobbed up and down. "Mrs. K. lets me help her. She said we can make a pie this time. Mr. K. tells me stories about princes."

Justin felt guilty that his daughter never had grandparents who could give her that special love and attention. But the Keenans were good surrogates.

"I'm glad we both like it," he told her.

"Do you like Morgan, too?" she asked.

"Yes, I do." He had to admit the small-town mayor had been disturbing his thoughts far too much over the last four days. He kept telling himself that he didn't want to get involved in a relationship, especially with someone he'd be working with, and someone who had permanence written all over her.

He thought back to the nightly phone calls. When the business was concluded, their conversations had not. Over the phone, Morgan had been relaxed, easier with talking about herself. Maybe it was the fact that there had been some three hundred and eighty miles between them.

That was what stumped him. She wasn't shy, unless he got personal, then she pulled away.

"Daddy, we're here," Lauren called out. "Mr. K. is on the porch."

Justin pulled into a parking space and climbed out of the car. "Hello, Tim."

"Hi, Justin," Mr. Keenan called as he came down the steps. "Glad you made it back safe and sound." He immediately went to the rear of the car and opened the door for Lauren.

"Welcome back, Princess Lauren." He bowed. "May I help you out of your carriage?"

Justin watched as his daughter cupped her hands over her mouth and giggled.

Tim sent him a wink. "I used to play this game with my girls." He grew serious. "While you were out in the storm, the pretending helped to distract her."

As Tim reached in the back seat, Justin looked toward the porch. Morgan came out the door and his own excitement caught him off guard.

She had on a long skirt and a blouse with a green sweater hanging over her hips. Her glorious red hair glistened in the sunlight, lying in curls against her shoulders. He doubted she had any idea how beautiful she looked standing there. She glowed with a natural beauty that made him ache.

Justin followed Tim and Lauren along the walk and up the steps to the porch. His throat was suddenly dry.

"Hello, Morgan," he managed to say as their hands touched, sending a heated current through him.

"Justin." She nodded. "How was your trip?"

He reluctantly let her hand slip from his. "The weather cooperated." He lowered his voice. "So did my daughter."

Morgan smiled, then turned to his daughter. "Welcome back, Lauren." She clasped the child's mitten-covered hands. "I should say, welcome home."

Lauren's eyes lit up. "My daddy and me are going to live in a big house, for ever and ever."

"How about that." Morgan glanced back at Justin and their gazes locked. "But you're going to stay here with us for a while—aren't you?"

"I know, it's gonna be fun," Lauren said excitedly. "I get to go to school." Suddenly a panicked look changed her expression. "But I don't know any kids."

Tim Keenan came to the rescue. "I forgot to tell you, princess, there's going to be a tea party tomorrow. Seems there are some little girls who want to meet you."

"Really?" Lauren wiped her eyes.

Justin watched as the burly man gently soothed his daughter's fears and a smile reappeared on her face.

"Daddy, we're going to have a party 'cause all the little girls want to meet me."

"That's wonderful, sweetie." He looked at Tim and mouthed a "thank you."

Tim pulled him aside. "Don't thank me. It was Morgan's idea." Then Mr. K. took Lauren's hand and walked her through the door. "Come on, Mrs. K. has lunch ready for all of us."

"Claire, you didn't need to go to any trouble," Justin said.

"When you get to know my wife, you'll realize that she loves to cook," Tim told him. "And that family and friends eat in the kitchen. So you'll join us?"

"Thank you. We'd love to," he said.

Tim walked off with Lauren, and Justin stayed back with Morgan.

"We should join them," she said.

"First, I want to talk with you."

Morgan found herself staring. He looked just as good as she'd remembered, dressed causally in his new attire of jeans and a sweater. He pulled off his navy peacoat and hung it on a hook.

Morgan was glad he was back. She had missed them both.

Justin reached for her hand but she resisted, pulling away. "I've missed you," he told her. "It surprised me…but I found myself thinking about you far too much."

She was thrilled and frightened at the same time.

He took a step closer. "I know this could complicate things, but I want to spend time with you, Morgan."

She tried to act calm. "I don't think it's a good idea…"

When her mother called to them, Morgan said, "We should go to lunch."

He frowned. "Okay, I'll let this go for now. Would you at least go with me this afternoon to meet the contractor at the house?"

She hesitated, torn between really wanting to see the old house and keeping away from Justin. She finally gave in. "Okay."

"Good." This time he took her hand. "And maybe later we can discuss why you keep running away from me."

She started to argue, but his grip tightened and all arguments were forgotten.

"At least tell me, are you glad I'm back?"

This time she didn't hesitate. "Yes, I'm glad you're back."

CHAPTER FIVE

Two hours later, with Lauren under the watchful eye of the Keenans back at the Inn, Justin and Morgan drove to Calloway Manor. They entered through huge double oak doors with an oval cut-glass pane.

Morgan hadn't seen the dirt and grime from years of neglect as she walked across the marble floor of the massive entry.

"It's beautiful," she said, wandering around in amazement. The arched staircase that circled the room was missing some of the railing, but that could be easily replaced. A crystal chandelier, laced with cobwebs, hung over a scarred pedestal table that had been left behind.

The walls were dingy, and the detailed woodwork incredible, but dull from lack of attention. She walked into the sitting room. The focal point was a set of bay windows that looked out onto the large yard and to the street. She walked to shredded sheer curtains, recalling her own lost dreams from her childhood.

I'm going to live in that big house, she'd told seven-year-old Paige. *I'm going to marry a handsome man, and have lots of babies. I'll be the best mom in the world. And I'm never, never going to leave my children.*

"Morgan…"

She jerked around. "Sorry. Did you say something?"

He came to her with a smile on his face. "I asked, how do you like the place?"

"I've always liked it." She glanced into the dining room with its detailed wainscoting and hardwood floors. The marble fireplace had a carved oak mantel. "That's a lie. I've always *loved* this house."

Justin glanced around. "I'm beginning to conjure up some serious feelings myself," he said. "It's a shame no one has lived here in so long."

"It's been close to ten years," she told him. "When I was about seven the Jarrell family moved here. He was an executive of the Sunny Haven Mine. They entertained a lot. Fancy parties, as we used to call them as kids."

"Did your family ever attend any of the parties?"

She wrinkled her nose. "Not hardly. The closest we got was when Paige and I sneaked out one night and hid in the bushes. I watched ladies in beautiful ball gowns get out of fancy cars. I couldn't wait until I would be old enough to go to my own ball."

She turned to him and saw he was smiling at her. "Sorry, I got carried away." Justin Hilliard had probably been to dozens of formal dances.

"Please, don't apologize." He sighed. "It's great to remember when life was so simple."

"Yeah, it ends so fast," Morgan said as the dark memory clouded her enthusiasm. She fought her sadness of the lost innocence.

His gray eyes met hers, concern laced with interest. "What happened, Morgan?" he prompted, his tone soft. "What happened to take your dreams away?"

Morgan tried to look away, but his gaze held her captive. "I grew up," she insisted. She wanted to get away, but she couldn't. Justin drew her. He made her feel things she hadn't let herself feel in a long time.

"But you can't stop dreaming," he said. "Nor living."

Before she got the chance to argue, his cell phone rang. She used the distraction to go into the kitchen.

Once again she was taken back in time. Although cabinet doors hung open and counters were nearly destroyed, the charm was still there. She walked to the breakfast nook and the windows that overlooked the backyard. Everything was barren outside, but she could picture it in the spring with colorful roses draped over the arbor, fragrant flowers in rows and freshly mown grass.

She felt Justin come up behind her. "That was the contractor. He got held up on another job so he won't be able to make it until tomorrow."

"Ben Harper is the best, so it's worth the delay."

"I missed you, Morgan. All week in Denver I kept telling myself that I should stay away from you…"

"Maybe you should," she whispered, feeling an ache for this man like nothing she'd ever felt before. "I can't get involved with you, Justin." But she didn't move away.

"Our lives can't always be about business."

"It's safer…" She didn't mean to say that. "Then no one gets hurt."

"The last thing I want is to hurt you, Morgan." He leaned in closer. "It's just that when I'm with you… there's this pull…this feeling…" Slowly he turned her around to face him, then brushed his mouth across hers.

Morgan sucked in a breath. Her pulse began pounding in an erratic rhythm as a sensation she'd never known made her heart dive into her stomach. Another feeling of warmth and awareness dismissed her fears…momentarily.

His lips moved over hers, caressing, tasting her, making her want more…and more. His tongue slipped inside and she found her own need surfacing. Her hands moved over his chest to around his neck and returned his fervor.

With a groan, Justin wrapped his arms around her and drew her closer, trapping her against him. Suddenly the familiar nightmare engulfed her like a stranglehold. She couldn't breathe.

She moaned and struggled to break free. "Please, don't."

"I apologize." He raised his hands in surrender. "I didn't mean…"

"No, I'm sorry." Her hands were trembling. "I told you I'm not any good at this."

He watched her for several heartbeats. "It's more than that, Morgan. What happened?"

"Nothing," she denied. "I want to leave."

Justin couldn't ignore her obvious terror, or reaction to him. "I can't forget it. The past four days, we've been talking over the phone. I thought…I thought there was something happening between us."

He started to reach for her, but seeing her fear, he dropped his arms. "Morgan, tell me…who hurt you so badly that you can't trust anyone else?"

Her eyes widened, then came the quick answer, "No one."

"Then why are you shaking? What have I done to make you fear me?" He started toward her. "And it's not because you don't want my touch… I've seen the desire in your eyes."

She shook her head. "We can't. We'll be working together."

"How can we work together if you're terrified of me?"

Tears pooled in her emerald eyes as she raised her chin in defiance. "If you'd rather have someone else handle…"

"No, I want you." He realized at that moment he wanted more than business from her…so much more. "I want to help you, Morgan." He lowered his voice. "I don't want to hurt you, but someone has… Please, tell me."

Morgan was so tired… All these years she'd fought the ghosts…the nightmares. The guilt. When she looked at Justin…she wanted so badly to go into his arms and let him hold her. "I can't."

"You can tell me anything. Pretend you're talking on the phone, and telling me about your childhood."

When she didn't say anything, he started using his own imagination. "Was it a guy? Some guy who treated you badly." He paced back and forth. "Tell me who…and I'll go after him and make him sorry he ever touched you."

She shook her head emphatically. "No, Justin. It's over… It happened a long time ago." A lone tear rolled down her cheek and she couldn't stop it. All the pain and anguish that churned up inside her, suddenly spilled out of her. "I…was raped."

Justin clenched his fists as her words echoed in his head. He wanted to hit something. Hard. Then he saw the look on Morgan's face, full of pain and anguish, and it made his heart ache. He fought to keep in control. His own anger wouldn't help. That wouldn't help her.

"I'm sorry, Morgan."

"Don't say that." She held up her hand. "I don't want your pity."

"You're not getting it. But no woman deserves to go through something that brutal. Just tell me the bastard is rotting in jail."

"Oh God, I can't believe I told you," Morgan whispered as she wiped the tears from her face and turned away. "We should go back to the Inn."

"They never caught him?"

She paused. "I…I never pressed charges."

He cursed under his breath. "You knew him?"

She didn't say anything, just walked to the window seat and sat down. "Like I said, it was a long time ago…in college. I'm fine now."

He went to her, aching to hold her. "You're not fine. Not when you tense up every time a man touches you."

"It was never a problem before…" She stopped her words.

Justin was thrilled at her near confession. "So do I make you want more? Do I make you feel things again?"

He'd never met a woman who talked less. "You make me feel things, too. Things I haven't felt in a long time." *And never with Crystal,* he added silently.

Her eyes widened. "Please don't say that."

"Why not? It's true." He leaned against the window ledge, surprised at his own admission. "I came here to get away from never being able to live up to my father's expectations, and the guilt that I couldn't keep my wife happy. My only concerns were myself and my daughter. Then you appeared." His eyes searched her beautiful face. "It was like a sucker punch to the gut. I want to see where this…you and me…goes."

She straightened. "It isn't a good idea…not when we need to put all our energy into the project."

He saw a flicker of interest along with her denial. "I have faith we can do both." He smiled. "But from the first time I saw you, I knew I wanted something more with you." He raised a hand. "I'll go as slow as you need to go."

"I've tried this before, Justin." She swallowed hard. "I get so far and I can't…" She closed her eyes for a moment. "This is so embarrassing." She sighed. "I can't give you what you need."

"You've given me more than you realize. But I want to help you to trust again… You trusted me enough to curl up next to me in the cave."

"I was trying to keep warm."

He pushed some more. "If you were honest, you'd admit it was more than that. Your body was doing more than stealing my warmth."

A blush rose over her cheeks and his heart soared.

"Answer me this, Morgan. Did you enjoy the kiss we just shared?"

"Maybe… But that doesn't mean you should kiss me again."

He folded his arms over his chest. "And I'm not going to."

She looked doubtful at his words.

"Believe it, Morgan. The next time we kiss, you're going to be the one who initiates it."

A twitch of a smile crossed her lips. "Oh, really? You're pretty sure of yourself."

"I'm pretty sure of you and that you can't resist my charm." He grew serious. "And you're pretty irresistible, yourself."

"Gee, thanks," she said with mock irritation.

"I could show you how I really feel about you, but you'd be running for the hills."

He took her hand. Somehow she'd get used to his touch, because he didn't plan to stop anytime soon.

"Just give me a chance."

By the next afternoon Morgan was even more frustrated by Justin Hilliard. He had to be the most distracting man she'd ever met. She knew what he was trying to do, and darn it, it was working.

Seated at the desk in her office, Morgan watched him in the tailored slacks and blue dress shirt with the sleeves rolled up his forearms. Justin looked as good in a suit as he had in jeans.

One thing was for sure, since yesterday's trip to Justin's newly acquired house, he hadn't mentioned or even approached her about anything personal.

It had been business as usual.

For him maybe, but not her. She hadn't been able to sleep at all last night, reliving the kiss, his touch. Her gaze went to his mouth. He had a great mouth and knew how to use it. A sudden heat began churning deep inside her stomach.

"Morgan…"

She blinked and refocused. "Sorry. What did you say?"

A glimmer of a smile caught her eye just before he pointed to the written proposal on her desk. "I asked how well you knew the work of this contractor…R & G Construction. They've never worked on a project this large, but they're from Durango." Those silver-gray eyes searched hers. "And I know you'd like to hire local workers if possible."

She regained some of her composure. "Only if they're the best. Maybe this time we should rely on experience." Her gaze met his.

"Just because they aren't experienced doesn't mean they can't do good work. Maybe we should divide the work. R & G Construction could do the strip mall and a Denver based company handle the hotel. What do you think?"

She wished she could concentrate. "Sounds like a good idea."

"Do you have a problem with using my project manager, Marc Rhodes?" he asked.

"No. He's worked for you before."

"He's the best. He'll bring this project in on time and on budget."

"I like that. Looks like he's the person for the job. Could you get me Mr. Rhodes résumé before the next council meeting?"

Justin nodded as he jotted down some notes. "Looks like that's all for now." He checked his watch. "I wonder how Lauren's tea party is going."

Morgan was surprised and pleased that in the midst of business he thought of his child. She glanced down at their agenda, seeing they'd finished. "Probably fine, but if you want to run back to the Inn and see for yourself, go ahead."

"I don't want to intrude on her party." He raised an eyebrow. "I was told it's for *girls* only."

Morgan suddenly thought of a solution. "I know a way you can see how she's doing without her seeing you."

"You have some secret passage into the dining room?"

"I guess you'll have to wait and see." She stood and headed for the door. "Are you going to follow me?"

He tossed her a sexy smile. "Anywhere."

* * *

"And we're going to live in a big house at 300 Birch Street," Lauren told the cute blond girl across the miniature table set up for today's party. "We can't move in yet 'cause it needs to be fixed up. And I'm going to have my room painted pink and I get to have a sleepover."

Justin stood inside the converted closet that at one time provided access for the waiter. The roll door was raised a few inches, just enough to see the four five-year-old girls: Lauren, Delaney, Mary Elisabeth and Sarah.

He glanced at Morgan next to him. "I don't remember agreeing to a sleepover," he whispered.

"Lauren has to have a sleepover, if not, she'll be a social outcast."

Justin groaned. "You're kidding?"

Morgan shook her head and fought a smile as she glanced back through the slit in the window. "She's also the new kid in town, and trying to make friends."

Justin knew how hard all the changes had been on Lauren. Suddenly more girlish laughter broke out and his heart swelled at the sound. "Then she'll have the best sleepover ever…and you can help me."

"Me?" Morgan gasped as she straightened in the closet area.

It smelled slightly musty, but with a mixture of Morgan's familiar citrus scent. Who would think the combination would be so intoxicating?

"You're better equipped than me," he whispered. "You're a woman." *Yes, she definitely was that.*

Justin stood there, staring at her. After Morgan's

admission yesterday, he hadn't been able to sleep. His own anger had kept him tossing and turning most of the night.

So many times during the day he'd wanted to go to Morgan and comfort her, but knew she was a strong, independent woman. He also knew how much courage it took for her to tell him she'd been raped.

"Well, I should get back to City Hall," she said.

"Don't go yet," he blurted out.

She stopped. "Is there some more business we need to discuss?"

"No, I just want to spend time with you," he admitted, feeling as awkward as a teenager.

"Justin…"

"Have dinner with me tonight."

She glanced over her shoulder. "You don't need to take me out because you feel…"

"Please don't say it's because I feel sorry for you," he finished for her. "You think this is a pity date? Hardly. Spending time with you is for my *own* selfish reasons. I feel good being with you." His gaze moved to her full mouth. "And I want you to know how beautiful and desirable you really are." She looked surprised. "Maybe you aren't ready to hear it now, Morgan, but I'm going to be around." He tossed her a grin. "And I thought if we went out on a date it would be a good opportunity for you to kiss me."

"Excuse me…you thought I would kiss you?"

He nodded. "I know when a woman likes my kisses and you do."

"That is so arrogant."

"No. It's truthful. Have dinner with me so you can get to know me better."

She blew out a long breath. "I'm not sure that's wise."

"Come on, Morgan. It's just dinner. Nothing is going to happen unless you start it."

She was thinking about it. "People will talk, Justin. They'll label us a couple. There are people in town who would like to use that against me."

"You're allowed to have a private life."

She didn't answer for a while, then said, "What about Lauren?"

He opened his mouth when he heard, "Daddy, what are you and Morgan doing in the closet?"

He swung around to find four little girls standing in the doorway, giggling. Darn if he didn't feel like he'd been caught doing something wrong.

"Uh, Morgan and I were looking for something."

More giggles. He loved that sound. "Is your tea party over?"

Lauren nodded. "It was so fun, Daddy. Mrs. K. made little cakes and sandwiches, and we had real raspberry tea."

"I hope you thanked Mrs. K."

Her dark head bobbed up and down. "A lot of times. Daddy, these are my new friends, Sarah, Mary Elisabeth, and Delaney."

"It's very nice to meet you, girls."

They waved shyly at him.

"Daddy, Delaney's mommy invited all of us to a

sleepover tonight." She drew in a breath and cupped her small hands together. "Can I go, please? Please."

He glanced at Morgan. "I don't know her parents."

Morgan knew the pretty divorced blonde, and no doubt Justin would get the opportunity, too. She hated the fact that she cared. "Delaney's mother is Kaley Sims. She went to school with Paige."

"Does she work at the real estate office?"

Morgan nodded. "She moved back here last year."

The little blonde, Delaney, spoke up. "We live with Grandma cause my daddy and mommy aren't married anymore."

Justin knelt down. "Well, I'm sure your grand-mother is happy you came to live with her."

"She watches me when Mommy works. She said I can have a sleepover 'cause Lauren is going to live here. So can she?"

"I think that's so sweet of your grandmother. And yes, Lauren can spend the night."

All the girls started jumping up and down cheering, then set off down the hall toward the stairs. Morgan saw the panicked look on Justin's face.

"I'll go help her pack her things," she said.

"I'd appreciate that," he said. "Then when you come down we'll discuss where to go for dinner."

"I haven't agreed…"

"But you want to, so tell me what kind of food you like?" He followed her to the staircase where he stopped as she corralled the girls and continued up.

"What's your favorite food?" he called after her, but she ignored him.

"It's Mexican."

He turned to find Claire Keenan standing in the hall.

"Oh, Mrs. Keenan, I want to thank you for all you've done for Lauren. She loved the party."

"It was our pleasure." She sighed, her soft eyes crinkled with a smile. "Sure brought back a lot of memories. Morgan was big on tea parties and playing princess. She was big on pretending." The older woman shook her head. "They grow up so fast."

He chuckled. "Sometimes I think Lauren just turned thirty overnight. It was good to hear her laugh."

"She's a beautiful child."

"And I can't thank you enough for all the help. I didn't realize how complicated raising a little girl can be."

"You seem to be doing just fine." Her smile grew. "And not so bad with the big girls, either. There's a great Mexican restaurant in Durango called Francisco's. It's Morgan's favorite."

"Thanks for the tip." He paused, wanting Morgan's family to know his plans. "Just so you know, tonight and this dinner has nothing to do with business. It's personal between me and Morgan."

CHAPTER SIX

THREE hours later, Lauren was at Delaney's house with all her new friends while Morgan sat with Justin in the corner booth of the candlelit restaurant, Francisco's.

Justin looked gorgeous dressed in his wine-colored sweater, emphasizing those broad shoulders of his.

And he kept looking at her, smiling.

"Have I told you how lovely you look?"

Morgan felt herself blush. "Yes, and thank you... again."

Paige should get all the credit for how she looked for her date. Once her sister had heard about her evening with Justin, she'd rushed over with an off-the-shoulder black angora sweater and a pair of slate-gray pleated slacks. The hairstyle was her idea, too. Morgan's long hair was pulled back from her face with clips. Paige then added makeup, eye shadow and lip liner. Too bad her sister couldn't do anything to cure her nervousness. Which was silly; it was only a dinner.

Justin watched Morgan. He'd tried everything to ease her tension, but nothing seemed to work.

"You know two people who spent a night in a cave, and an afternoon in a closet, shouldn't be acting like strangers."

She blinked. "We didn't spend an afternoon in a closet. It was only about twenty minutes."

"I apologize. Maybe it was just me wishing it were longer." He leaned closer. "You're very hard to resist, Morgan."

She took another sip of her wine.

"Don't get panicked, I'm only being honest, Morgan. I care about you, and I think you're attracted to me." When she started to argue, he raised his hand. "But since I'm making you feel uncomfortable maybe we should work on our friendship, discuss something else." He thought a moment. "Ben Harper came by the house this afternoon. He's agreed to take on the Hilliard Manor project."

"Oh, Justin, that's wonderful. How soon before he begins?"

"The end of the week. He's going to start restoring upstairs. Painting and some repair work to the master suite and two other bedrooms. One will be an office and the other Lauren's room. He says he needs two weeks to make the bedrooms and a bath livable."

"I bet Lauren is excited."

"She doesn't know, yet." His gaze raised to her green eyes. "You're the first person I've told." He realized Morgan was the one he wanted to tell. "I need your expertise, too. Would you help me choose some paint colors?"

"Shouldn't you hire a decorator?"

"I want the place to look like a home, not a museum. Your mother said you handled redecorating of the guest rooms. I especially like the colors in your shop and your quilt. Is blue your favorite color?"

She nodded.

"I have a fondness for blue, too." He reached for her slender hand, examining her long fingers. "Okay, maybe it's tall redheads who like blue." He took a chance and laced his fingers with hers.

"You can't paint your entire house blue," she whispered.

He leaned closer. "Maybe not. What would you paint the rooms?"

She gave a shuddering breath when his fingers stroked the back of her hand. "Yellow…for the kitchen. Maybe a pale yellow for Lauren's room… No, it should be pink."

Her gaze met his, and he rejoiced to see the spark of desire in those green depths.

"What about my bedroom, Morgan?"

Her full lips parted, and her breathing grew a little labored. "I…I haven't seen your bedroom."

Justin fought back a groan as he conjured up images of them together. "I guess I'll have to show it to you." Leaning toward her, he whispered, "We could stop by tonight on the way back to the Inn."

"It'll be late," she protested weakly.

It was already too late for him. "Ten minutes," he told her. "I promise all we'll do is just look at the room." He locked his gaze on her. "Unless…you have other ideas. You're in the driver's seat. I'm not going to make the first move on you, Morgan. That will be up to you."

During the drive back from dinner in Durango, Morgan let Justin Hilliard talk her into stopping at the house. Of course, since she hadn't gone upstairs the other day, she jumped at the chance now.

Well, she'd show him it was still going to be business between them, no matter how much the man distracted her.

And she was only giving him five minutes.

Justin unlocked the door and turned on the light in the entry. "A crew is coming by tomorrow to clean up the place and rope off part of the downstairs from Lauren while they're working." He took her hand and led her to the stairs. "It's going to be a while before they finish remodeling the kitchen. So it looks like we'll be cooking with a microwave for a few months."

"But it will be well worth it in the end," she told him.

At the top of the stairs, he flicked on another set of lights, illuminating the hallway that led them past four bedrooms. The one at the end of the corridor was the master suite. He reached inside the double doors and turned on the overhead light, a crystal teardrop chandelier.

Morgan's eyes adjusted to the sudden brightness and she took a step into the huge, empty room. Hardwood floors made an echoing sound as she walked to the marble fireplace framed with a dark wood stained mantel. A window seat made a cozy area overlooking the back of the house. She went into the dressing area, and the large walk-in closet.

"This is wonderful. So much room."

"Give you any ideas?"

She swung around to see him sitting on the window seat, his arms crossed over his chest. *He* gave her ideas all right. A shiver went through her. Surprised, she quickly shook away her wandering thoughts.

"What does your furniture look like?"

"I don't know. I'm going to furnish this house with everything new. You have any thoughts on what style of bed I should have?"

"Big. In this size room it needs it. And masculine…"

"Whoa…I don't want it too masculine. I'm hoping I'm not going to be living in here all by myself…"

Morgan couldn't look at him. Of course, he wanted a woman. A normal, healthy man like Justin would want a woman to share his bed. She just wasn't that woman. "I should get back to the Inn." She started out when he stopped her.

"Are you going to keep running from what you want?"

She paused at the door, and looked over her shoulder. "And what exactly do I want?"

Even from across the room, his heated gaze reached her. "A loving relationship with a man who cares about you. You want me."

She could only blink at his arrogance.

"Of course, no more than I want you."

"Look, Justin, just because you learned about my past…and you made a silly bet about a kiss, doesn't give you the right…"

"I think it gives me every right. I care about you, Morgan. I didn't plan to, but it happened and I want to see where it could go with us."

Suddenly she found she wanted to, too. But she was frightened. What if she never could be what he wanted…and needed? "I can't…"

"Yes, you can. I'm right here to help you."

"I did try when you kissed me, but I had to pull away when you tried to hold me…"

"Maybe you weren't ready for that much contact. And I held you too tight," he finished for her. "So you take charge, Morgan. You kiss me."

Morgan gripped the doorknob, feeling a rush of excitement. She wanted to. She wanted to be the woman he wanted…he needed.

He arched an eyebrow. "You run a town, you own a business and you're going to head a large development project, and you're telling me you can't give me one little kiss?"

She didn't answer.

"Just tell me this, Morgan. Do you want to kiss me?"

Her heartbeat shot off pounding. "Yes…"

"Show me," he challenged in a husky, rough voice. "I'll sit here. I won't even put a hand on you."

She tried not to be affected, but felt the pull.

"I dare you, Morgan. I dare you to kiss me."

She took the first step, then the second and realized she had to keep herself from going too fast. "This is crazy."

She stopped in front of him, telling herself that she was doing this just to shut him up. As if taking medicine, she braced herself for the worst. She placed her hands on his broad shoulders, feeling his strength. She leaned down, and placed her mouth against his. His lips were warm and firm. The slow awareness began to curl in her stomach as her mouth moved tentatively over his. She pulled away, her heart drumming in her chest as she looked into his pewter gaze.

"Again, Morgan," he breathed. "Kiss me again."

His husky words made her daring, or it was just the fact she couldn't seem to resist him. This time she grew bolder, hungrier as her hands moved to his hair, combing through the dark thickness as her mouth caressed and stroked his. She finally pulled back, but only inches, so she could study his incredible mouth.

"Again…" he breathed.

Justin Hilliard was quickly growing addictive. He made her feel things. Good things, but scary nonetheless. Her mouth pressed to his, and this time, she felt his tongue running along the seam of her lips. On a soft moan, she opened to him, then heard him groan and delve deeper inside to taste her.

"That's it, green eyes. Let me taste you."

Quickly Morgan became lost in the pleasure he made her feel. She'd never, ever experienced anything like this…and she wanted more.

"Justin..." she breathed against his mouth. "I've never...never..."

"Excuse me," said a voice from the doorway.

Morgan swung around and saw her brother-in-law, Sheriff Reed Larkin.

"I'm sorry, Morgan...Justin." Reed looked as embarrassed as she felt. "We got a call that there was activity in the house." He rubbed his forehead. "It...means someone was inside. I had to check it out."

"It's okay, Sheriff," Justin said as he stood up, but kept Morgan close. "I was showing Morgan around upstairs."

Reed nodded. "Sorry for the intrusion, I'll be leaving. Have fun." He winked and disappeared.

Morgan was mortified. "This is so embarrassing."

"Why? So what if your brother-in-law caught us kissing? I'm sure he and Paige have done their share."

"You don't understand." She paced. "The entire family is going to find out."

"And that's bad because..."

"Because I told you, I'm not good at...this."

He raised an eyebrow at her. "The way you were kissing me, you could have fooled me."

Morgan gasped. "That's only because of the things you were saying."

He smiled. "You mean because I was encouraging you?"

She nodded.

"It worked because we both wanted to keep on kissing."

edge that the tender feelings she had nursed for Brian Mellor

She got that strange feeling in her stomach again. She wanted it, too. "There will come a time when you want more."

He frowned. "Morgan, no one has a right to make you do anything that you don't want to do."

Justin fought to hide his anger at the man who'd done this to her. He took her hand and led her back to the window seat to sit down, and searched her face. "And I might not like it, but if you say no, that means no."

Her gaze stayed on their clasped hands for a long time, then she finally raised her head. Her chin trembled and tears welled in her eyes. "After what happened with Ryan…he said I'd been teasing him for too long…and it was bound to happen."

Justin cursed, wanting to find the person who'd done this to her. "He lied, Morgan. It wasn't your fault. No matter how he explained it, he took what you weren't willing to give him." He wanted to wrap his arms around her and just hold her…absorb her pain and the guilt she'd carried all these years.

"I'm not him, Morgan." Taking a chance, Justin raised his hand and touched her cheek. "You're too precious to me to ever hurt you like that. When we get together, I want you to want me as much as I want you."

Her eyes rounded. "But what if I can't…"

He smiled. "I'm willing to wait for that day."

The next morning, Morgan went down to breakfast at her usual time. With Justin as a guest here, she didn't have any choice but to face him.

I'm willing to wait for that day, he'd told her. She'd stayed awake most of the night, reliving his words and the kisses they'd shared. Although her experiences had been limited, she'd never before felt this close to a man. But it was different than when she was with Ryan. For one, she was older now. Although Ryan came from an affluent family, Justin had never thrown around his wealth. Never made her feel that they didn't fit together.

It would be so easy to fall in love with the man, but being the woman he needed was another story.

Hearing some commotion, she hurried down the back stairs that led into the kitchen where her parents, were seated at the table with Justin and Lauren.

Lauren spotted her first. "Morgan! You're here." The girl ran over to meet her, her dark ponytails swinging back and forth. "I'm going to kindergarten. It's my first day."

"That's right it is. Are you excited?"

The child nodded. Dressed in a pair of jeans and a pink blouse and matching sweater, she looked adorable.

"Delaney and Mary Elisabeth get to go on the bus, but I can't 'cause Daddy wants to take me."

Morgan stole a look at the terrible father who wanted the pleasure of taking his child to her first day of school. He was dressed in his uniform of late: jeans and a green crew-neck sweater. Her attention went to his freshly shaven face, and his mouth, and suddenly she recalled his heart-stopping kisses. His silver gaze locked with hers and he smiled.

She glanced away. "Well, looks like you have a problem." She hesitated a minute, then came up with a solution. "Your daddy just wants to make sure you're happy in your new school, and meet your teacher. So maybe it would be okay—just this once—if your daddy drives you. And so he can take pictures for your scrapbook, and then you can ride the bus home with your friends."

The five-year-old pursed her cute mouth. "I guess that's okay." She turned and walked to her father. "Daddy, you can take me to school today."

"Thank you, sweetie." He looked at Morgan and she had trouble catching her breath. "And thank you," he whispered as he walked by. "I'll see you later."

Morgan worked to regain her composure as she helped Lauren on with her backpack. Then she was rewarded with a hug from the child. "Bye, Morgan."

"Bye, Lauren. You have a good day in school."

The girl hugged both the Keenans, then father and daughter left. Morgan went to the coffeemaker and poured herself a cup. When she returned to the table, her parents were watching her.

"What?"

"I was just thinking what a sweet little girl Lauren is," her father said. "She reminds me a lot of you when you were that age. She knows exactly what she wants…and goes after it."

"And Justin is such a good father," her mother added.

Here it comes, Morgan thought as she drank her fresh coffee.

"And he's such a handsome man. It's a shame he's all alone." Her mother glanced at her. "How was your date last night, honey?"

She wanted to deny it wasn't really a date, but it was. "It was fine."

Her mother raised an eyebrow. "Just fine?"

Tim Keenan placed his hand over his wife's. "Claire…Morgan doesn't want to talk about it. I think we should respect that."

Morgan discovered she wanted to tell them all about how much fun she'd had being with Justin, how he made her feel. But at this point, she didn't trust her own feelings.

"Mother, we have to work together. Our first concern has to be the project. There isn't any time for much else."

"That's a shame because both you and Justin could use a life outside work. Of course, if there aren't any sparks between the two of you…" Her mother took a sip of her coffee. "By the way, Paige called earlier. She said Reed ran into you and Justin last night at the Holloway house." Claire Keenan smiled. "So…you're taking Justin up on helping him decorate his place."

Morgan groaned. This was exactly what she was afraid of. "I kind of got talked into it."

Later that morning, Morgan was in her office, but the work on her desk sat untouched. She hadn't been able to concentrate. There was a knock on the door and Justin peered in. "You got a minute?"

Morgan's stomach took a dip, quickly sending

her off balance, but she pulled herself together. Here was the reason why she couldn't focus. She gave him a nod as she came around the desk.

"Were we scheduled for a meeting?"

Justin closed the door behind him. "No, I just wanted to see you and thank you."

"Thank me…?" Why couldn't she form a sentence?

His smile brightened. "For this morning. Lauren was insistent about going on the bus until you convinced her otherwise."

Her attention went to his mouth. More memories of his gentle touches and soft kisses flashed through her mind, causing a shiver to go through her. She quickly pushed them away. "I…I hope you got a lot of pictures."

He nodded. "With her friends, teacher, even the class fish tank."

They both laughed. He sobered first. "I enjoyed being with you last night."

"So did I."

"Good. I hope we can do it again."

"I'm not so sure it's a good idea." Morgan walked back to her desk. Justin followed her.

"I see. Any particular reason that you've changed your mind since last night? I thought you were willing to give us a chance."

She remained silent.

Justin knew there was chemistry between them, more than he'd ever felt with any other woman he'd been with. He wasn't about to let her give up on them. "You're going to have to explain this to me."

She finally turned around. "It's not the kisses. I don't want to lead you on… What if I can't go any farther…than kissing."

Oh, he wanted more, all right. "I told you, you set the pace."

He took her hand and loved the fact that she didn't pull away when he touched her. "We're going to erase all those bad memories, Morgan. I meant what I said about helping you. It started last night when you kissed me…and kissed me."

She closed her eyes, and he noticed a change in her breathing. She wanted him, too.

"Intimacy between a man and a woman can be a beautiful thing, Morgan. And I want to be the one to show you." He sank down to sit on the edge of the desk. He tugged on her hand. "Now, I need you to kiss me."

"How can you be so sure about this?"

"About the kiss?" he tried to tease as he brought her hand to his pounding heart.

"No, about us being…together."

"About me making love to you?" he asked as he watched her eyes light up, and her cheeks flush pink. "Because I think you want it as much as I do." He rushed on. "Maybe not as soon as I do, but I'm going to wait until you do. I care about you, Morgan."

"I care about you, too." She frowned. "I'm just afraid that if I mess this up that it will affect us working together."

"We actually won't be working together much. Marc Rhodes will be the hands-on person for the resort. He's more than capable of handling the job. I meant what I said about having time for Lauren… and myself. I've spent a lot of years working eighty-hour weeks. No more." His grip on her hand tightened. "It's going to be all about family and enjoying life. But that won't stop us from spending time together."

Morgan was standing so close. It tormented him to have her that near and not be able to kiss her. If she knew his true feelings she'd run so fast…

"I'm afraid, for now, I'll be spending most of my time at the house," he told her. "Lauren needs her own space, and so do I."

"You're so good with her, Justin."

He grew serious. "I wasn't always. It's taken me a long time to get my priorities straight. It's time she has a real home."

"Do you still want my help?"

"Oh, yes. I'm headed there today and thought you could come along. You can start on the wall colors."

There was a knock on the door and she drew her hand from his and went to answer it. It was her secretary with some papers for Morgan to sign.

"I have a meeting in a few minutes for the upcoming Western Days in two weeks. But I could stop by in about an hour." She glanced at the clock. "When do you have to pick up Lauren?"

"Not until three. She's going to Delaney's house for the afternoon." He sighed. "I'm not used to Lauren being so independent."

"That's because she's thriving, and happy."

"And you and your family have to take credit for a lot of that."

"Her daddy should take some credit, too." She went to him, lifted up on her toes and planted a long, lingering kiss on his surprised mouth. She pulled back and smiled. "And you have a way with women."

CHAPTER SEVEN

ABOUT noon that day, Morgan arrived at the Hilliard house with lunch. Stepping up on the worn planked porch floor, she grew nervous in anticipation of seeing Justin. Somehow, in just a few short weeks, she'd let him get to her.

She'd become far too eager to share his enticing kisses. Not long ago the man was a stranger, but even then she'd ended up spending the night with him in a cave, sleeping in his arms. And every time she'd set foot in this house she managed to end up kissing him.

Instead of reaffirming her resolve to stay away, she felt a little thrill, wondering just how Justin would persuade her today.

Morgan opened the front door to the sound of a power saw coming from the second floor. She climbed the stairs and walked down the hall to the second bedroom. There was a man leaning over the makeshift worktable propped upon sawhorses. Justin. He was running his power saw over a sheet of plywood.

Faded jeans encased his narrow hips and a carpenter's tool belt hung even lower. A form-fitting black T-shirt stretched over his broad shoulders and back. His ebony hair was messy and sprinkled with sawdust. Sexy didn't begin to describe him.

When the saw stopped, he looked up and smiled.

He had her heart pounding without even saying a word.

"Well, hello." He put down his tool and came toward her.

"Hi..." She tried to steady her breathing. Impossible.

He took the bags of food from her and set them on the floor. "I know you can give a better greeting than that." He took a step closer.

Morgan swallowed. Seeing the desire in his eyes, she couldn't seem to stop herself. She leaned in and placed her mouth on his. She was about to pull away when he groaned and began to deepen the kiss. So much for willpower. Following his lead, she opened to his passion with her own. She pressed her hands against his chest to keep space between them, but instead slid them up over his hard chest and around his neck.

This time she whimpered as his tongue dipped into her mouth, teasing and tasting her. She boldly returned the favor as her fingers tangled in his hair and held him close. She was quickly getting lost in the pleasure when Justin broke off the kiss.

He rested his forehead against hers. "Wow. We'd better slow down a little."

"Oh…" Morgan took a step back when Justin reached for her hand.

"No…don't pull away, green eyes," he told her.

The last thing Justin wanted was to discourage Morgan's advances. "I love what you're doing. It just was a little…intense." He grimaced at her. "And I'm just a guy who wants you very much." He was a little disappointed when she didn't admit to anything.

She pointed to the bags. "I brought you lunch."

"Maybe it's a good idea if we concentrate on that." He picked up one of the sacks and looked inside. "Do I smell pastrami?" When she nodded, he said, "My favorite."

She finally relaxed. "Good, I wasn't sure what you liked."

"I'm pretty easy. There isn't much I don't like." He carried the food to the window seat and Morgan followed with the drinks.

She took out the foam cups of iced tea and sat down. "Are you working as a carpenter now?"

"No, I'm making the shelves for Lauren's doll collection." He took a big bite of his sandwich and chewed. "This is great!"

"Just so you know, we have an excellent deli here in town. One of the fringe benefits."

Justin stopped eating and stared at her. His pulse raced just with her close. "There are a lot of benefits in this town, starting with the beautiful mayor."

She glanced away. "Thank you."

The shame of it was, Morgan Keenan didn't think she was beautiful, and she did everything she could think of to keep other people from seeing it. "You don't have to thank me. It's the truth." He leaned toward her, aching to touch her. "Your skin is flawless, all creamy with just enough freckles across your nose. Oh, and your long, slender neck, that begs to be kissed. But it's those green eyes of yours that cause my heart to stop every time I look at you…"

"You shouldn't say…"

He cocked an eyebrow. "I shouldn't tell you the truth? Why not? You're a lovely woman, Morgan Keenan. And you make me feel things that I've never felt before…with any woman."

She hesitated. "But…you were married."

He refused to feel guilty about Crystal any longer. "Yes, I was married. And I won't speak badly of my ex-wife because she's gone." His gaze held hers. "Crystal and I weren't good together. That's the shame of it. We both needed different things out of our marriage. We'd been divorced for over a year before she died." He hated to spoil the mood, but he wanted Morgan to know about his past.

"Lauren suffered the worst." He smiled sadly. "That's the main reason I want to give her a good home life… I didn't have it growing up with my father, but Lauren will."

Morgan picked at the crust on her sandwich, hearing Justin tell her how much he wanted a family, a wife and children. She still wasn't sure if she could give him that. Yet, she found she wanted to try at having a relationship with a man. This man. He cared about her feelings, and he'd helped her with her fears. That gave her the courage to ask. "Justin, you know that meeting I had to go to this morning?"

He nodded and continued chewing his food.

"It was for our Western Days celebration in a few weeks. Friday night is Miss Kitty's Saloon Casino Night, and on Saturday there's a Sadie Hawkins dance."

"Sadie Hawkins, huh. Isn't that the dance where the woman asks the man?"

Morgan nodded this time.

"Are you trying to warn me that a lot of desperate single women are going to be pursuing me?"

"Could be." She laughed, then quickly sobered. "But it's this woman who is asking you. Justin, would you like to go to the dance with me?"

He raised an eyebrow. "So you're going to save me from all the others?"

She found it easy to play along. "Do you want to be saved?" she asked.

"Only by you."

She swallowed hard. "So you'll go with me?"

He nodded slowly. "But only if I get a kiss to seal the deal."

"You drive a hard bargain, Justin Hilliard." She placed her sandwich down on its wrapper and leaned toward him, finding she was eager to comply.

"Well, I have to take advantage of any opportunities."

"You're wrong, Mr. Hilliard." She slipped her hands around his neck and whispered, "This is my opportunity."

She brushed a kiss across his mouth and pulled away, then returned. This time she nibbled on his lower lip to hear him groan. She didn't wait for him to take the initiative, she teased his mouth with her tongue, then delved inside.

By the time she broke away he was breathing hard. His eyes met hers.

"You're just full of surprises, Mayor."

"Daddy, I like that pink the best," Lauren said as she pointed to one of the many sample colors on the bedroom wall. "Morgan said it's called Cotton Candy. It's my favorite. Delaney likes it, too."

The two five-year-olds nodded in agreement.

It had been over a week since the workmen had started on the house, and things were moving fast. After several samples had been applied to the wall, his daughter had finally decided on one. Justin smiled. It was the brightest pink from the many samples Morgan had chosen. "If you're really sure, then I'll have it painted tomorrow."

"Yes, Daddy, I'm really, really sure." Lauren cheered as both girls jumped up and down. "Then can I have a sleepover?"

He'd been afraid of this. "You don't even have a bed yet."

"Daddy, we can use sleeping bags." Those big blue eyes gave him a hopeful look. "Please…"

They were a week from even moving in. "We'll talk about it later."

"Okay, but don't forget," she reminded him. The

doorbell rang. "Delaney's mom is here." The two girls charged out of the room, their footsteps echoing down the hall.

Justin rubbed his forehead. Between the meetings about the resort, and trying to get the house livable, he wasn't sure what was going on. Of course, Lauren's room took priority over everything else.

Suddenly he heard voices and he looked toward the door. The girls had returned, bringing with them a petite, blue-eyed blonde about thirty years old. Delaney's mother.

The woman boldly eyed him from head to toe, then a slow smile appeared on her ruby-colored lips. "Hello. I'm Kaley Sims. You must be Justin Hilliard."

"Yes, I am." He came across the room to shake her hand. "It's so nice to finally meet you, Mrs. Sims. I need to thank you and your mother for having Lauren over so much these past weeks."

"We love having her," she said. "Delaney and Lauren have become such good friends." She began playing with her blond hair. "It's hard when you're a single parent. Thank goodness for my mother's help. She's one of the reasons I moved back to Destiny."

"This town is a great place to raise a child."

Her smile widened. "So I see you're sold on small-town living. I thought maybe you were here only for the duration of the project."

"That's what brought me here, but this will be Lauren's and my home."

"Good, then we'll be seeing you around. Do you know about the upcoming Western Days celebration?"

"I've heard about it."

Kaley opened her mouth just when the girls started making a commotion. He and Kaley turned to see that Morgan had arrived.

Why did he feel as if he'd just been saved? "Morgan," he called and went to greet her.

Morgan's smile slowly faded when she saw Kaley. "Hello, Justin. Kaley."

"Hello, Morgan," the blonde said.

"Kaley just stopped by to pick up Delaney."

They all studied the two girls playing. "The two have been inseparable since the tea party," Justin said.

"That's all Delaney talks about." Kaley glanced back at Justin. "Like I was saying, there's Western Days next weekend."

"Morgan has been telling me all about it. A Sadie Hawkins dance." Justin knew what Kaley was about to ask and wanted to make it clear he had feelings for a certain mayor. "I haven't been to one of those since high school." He smiled at Morgan. "And thanks to Mayor Keenan it looks like I'm going to another."

"You're going?" Kaley said, unable to hide her surprise.

"Yes," Morgan said. "Justin's agreed to go with me."

The blonde eyed the couple, then said, "Well, that's nice. I'm not sure I'll be going this year, but I will be working the casino night." She gave Justin a sly smile. "Stop by my table and try your luck." She gathered up her daughter and walked out. Lauren went off to her bedroom.

"If you'd rather go with Kaley... I...can..."

He turned to Morgan, not believing what he was hearing. "Have I given you any reason to think that I'd rather go with Kaley?"

She shook her head.

"Good, because you're the only woman I want to be with. And quit looking at me like that, Morgan, or I'll break my promise and kiss you right here and now to prove it to you."

It surprised him that Morgan didn't give him a panicked look. Instead she turned to him and sighed. "Then I guess I'd better go talk to my sisters, because Kaley Sims needs to find a guy...of her own." Then she stood on her toes and placed a kiss on his mouth, surprising him once again.

Morgan knew she was acting crazy. But since Justin Hilliard had come to town, she'd been doing so many things that weren't like her. Her mouth moved over his, savoring his taste, a flavor that she'd become addicted to.

She finally broke off the kiss, but didn't retreat. She boldly looked into his eyes. "You're the only man I want to be with."

"You're not playing fair, green eyes." He took a step back. "We better change the subject...for now."

She nodded, realizing she wasn't ready to commit to much more than dating and kissing. But when the time came, would she be willing? She didn't know. All she knew was if the time came she wanted that man to be Justin.

"Okay, what brings you by the house?"

"I've talked with Marc Rhodes by phone. He wants to set up a meeting. When are you available?"

"I've made myself available in the morning until Lauren gets out of school."

"That should give us enough time."

He leaned toward her and lowered his voice. "There's never enough time when I'm with you. How about tonight? We can take Lauren out to dinner."

Morgan was excited that Justin thought of them as a couple. She was working on that, too. "How about you and Lauren come to family dinner at the Keenans—but be warned, my sisters and their husbands will be there. You'll probably be drilled with questions, at least by my lawyer sister, Paige."

Justin folded his arms across his chest, looking thoughtful. She knew that since he'd been living at the Inn, he'd refused to intrude on the weekly family get-together.

"I can handle it, but what I don't want is for you to feel pressured or uncomfortable."

He was leaving this up to her, too. He'd been so considerate and patient with her when most men would have walked away. "I won't. Not with you."

An hour later, Justin followed Morgan and Lauren into the Keenan kitchen, which was already crowded with the family. Claire and Tim Keenan were the first to greet them, the sisters exchanged kisses and hugs. All the affection was something Justin still had trouble getting used to. But not Lauren. She took hugs from everyone.

"Glad you could join us," Tim said.

"Thanks for having us. I know it was short notice."

"You and Lauren are always welcome here."

Reed walked to him. "How's the house coming along?"

"Fine. They're painting tomorrow morning. And the bedroom furniture arrives in a few days."

"And then we get to move in," Lauren said. "My room is gonna be Cotton Candy Pink. Morgan helped pick it out and I get to have a sleepover as soon as we move in."

"Whoa, sweetie. I told you we'd talk about the sleepover…later."

"Daddy, Mary Elisabeth and Delaney and Sarah already said they want to come." Her lower lip quivered. "I promised 'em."

Paige Keenan Larkin looked at him. "Yeah, Daddy, she promised. What's the matter—can't handle all those females?"

He grimaced. "You're right. I'm a bit concerned about dealing with four little girls. More to the point is that parents aren't crazy about their young daughters spending the night without any adult female in the house."

Paige rubbed her rounded stomach. "Oh, my," she breathed. "I guess I didn't think about that."

"That's hard to explain to a five-year-old, especially since all her new friends have invited her to their houses. I owe everyone."

"There's got to be a solution," Paige said, looking thoughtful. "I have an idea. Just a second." She hurried off, grabbed Leah's and Morgan's hands on the way to their mother at the stove and began to talk quietly.

"That can't be good," Holt said, nodding at the group of Keenan women. "Whenever they do that they're cooking something up. And it's not food."

Reed and Tim joined the men. "What did you say to Paige?"

After Justin told them, Holt said, "I can see your dilemma. Now, I'm doubly glad I have a boy. Corey loves sleeping on the ground." He frowned. "Of course Leah could be carrying a girl."

"Girls may be complicated, but they're worth the effort," Justin assured them. "Even with all the bows, ruffles and dolls, I wouldn't change a thing about Lauren."

"I'm going to be in the same boat," Reed said, and smiled. Justin knew Paige's baby was a girl. "I'm going to spoil my daughter rotten."

"Not if Paige has anything to say about it," Tim said as he arrived at the group. "Men, you have to be strong. The women in this family already have too much power."

Just then all four Keenan women turned to them and smiled. "I knew it, they're cooking something up," Reed said. "Paige already knows I can't say no to her. And believe me, she uses it against me."

"It's probably not so bad," Holt said, looking lovingly back at his pregnant wife.

Justin didn't care, either. Not when Morgan smiled at him.

Finally the women returned and Mrs. Keenan spoke. "We have an idea that might solve your problem, Justin."

"What problem?"

"The problem with Lauren and her sleepover," Claire said. "How about if you had Lauren bring her friends here?"

Justin flashed a glance at Morgan. "Oh, Claire, I can't ask you to do that."

"You didn't ask, we offered. Since your house isn't…equipped for girls, why not bring the girls here and have the sleepover on the third floor in the girls' old bedroom?"

Justin couldn't even absorb the idea before Lauren rushed over. "Oh, Daddy, please. Please, can we?"

"I still don't have a chaperone."

"Yes, you do," Morgan said. "I'll spend the night with the girls."

He couldn't believe that Morgan was doing this. "You really want to stay up all night with four five-year-olds?"

"I doubt they'll make it all night, but yes, it'll be fun. Unless you have a problem with it."

"Only that you'll be doing all the work."

"Oh, no. You're paying for the pizza." Morgan reached down and tickled Lauren.

"Yeah, Daddy, you have to buy us lots of pizza… and ice cream…and candy."

"Whoa, whoa." He raised a hand. "I don't want everybody getting sick."

Lauren grew serious. "Okay, a little ice cream and a little candy."

"That's better." He looked at Morgan. "Can I talk to you for a moment?"

Morgan glanced around the crowded room, wondering if she'd overstepped this time. "Sure." She led the way though the kitchen to the door and into the entry. "I'm sorry, Justin, I didn't mean to let Lauren overhear before you got the chance to decide."

"I'm not angry, Morgan. I just wanted to ask if you're sure about this. When I mentioned you helping with a sleepover, I was only kidding."

"I know, but I want to do it. And Mom agreed because there aren't any guests in the Inn right now. It's also the best solution to your…problem. It's very important Lauren fit in, Justin. She's in a new home…a new place… She needs this."

Justin stared at her for a long time and it was beginning to make Morgan nervous. Finally he said, "I wish I'd never made you that promise…"

"The promise?"

"The one where I said I wouldn't kiss you, because I want to…badly."

His confession thrilled her, and she discovered she wanted him to kiss her, too. Mindful that her family was close by, she leaned forward. "Then maybe I should put you out of your misery. Kiss me, Justin."

His gray eyes were dark with desire, then he smiled. "Oh, I know your plan. You think since your family is so close, I won't."

She hesitated, then said, "No, I'm hoping you will. Kiss me, Justin," she repeated.

"You have no idea how long I've been waiting to hear you say those words," he said as he reached out and placed his hands against her waist. "You sure you're okay with this?"

"Yes." And she was. So much so she that she stepped closer into the embrace. He leaned his head into hers and brushed a kiss against her mouth. She sucked in a breath, feeling the excitement, along with a warm tingle at his touch. He pulled back a little, his gaze questioning.

"Kiss me again," she breathed.

This time his hands cupped her face. "There's nothing I want more," he said as his head lowered and he captured her mouth, brushing his tongue over the seam of her bottom lip. She opened to him. Soon, they were both lost in the passion when she heard a gasp.

"Daddy, you're kissin' Morgan." Then Lauren's footsteps retreated, then came the distant sound of, "My daddy's kissing Morgan."

"Seems we've been discovered," she said, looking at him.

"Do you have a problem with that?"

She shook her head. "None whatsoever."

"I'm glad." He brought her hand to his lips and kissed it. "Come on, it's time to face the music. Together."

CHAPTER EIGHT

"I WANT my toes painted next," Delaney said, perched on one of the double beds in the Keenan sisters' old bedroom. It was nearly ten o'clock and there were no signs of any of the four five-year-olds' energy fading.

"Just let me finish Mary Elisabeth's first." Their toenails were so cute. Morgan finally finished her task and stood back to examine her work. All the girls were in pajamas and their hair had been styled. She also was dressed in flannel pajamas and the girls had given her a new hairstyle, too.

"I want Pink Diamonds," Delaney said. "Please."

Morgan went through the colors she'd purchased for tonight and found the bottle. All the girls watched as she applied the polish to the last toe. Once finished, she said, "Okay, you all have to sit quietly on the bed until it dries." She went to the television and put in *The Little Mermaid*.

Morgan blew out a breath as she looked at the four little angels seated along the bed. Their faces made up and their toes painted. Earlier they'd played dress-up with clothes and jewelry from an old chest in the attic. Thank goodness her mother hadn't thrown anything away. Then Justin had brought pizza and soda.

She was sure they'd had a good time because she was getting tired. She glanced at the clock to see it was after ten o'clock. Who would have thought that four tiny girls could have so much energy? Seeing the droopy-eyed children, Morgan hoped they'd fall asleep soon.

A soft knocking sound drew Morgan's attention. With the girls engrossed in the movie, she went to the door and found Justin standing in the dimly lit hallway. Her parents' bedroom was two doors down and they'd retired for the night.

"Hi," she whispered, and stepped out, pulling the door nearly closed behind her.

"How's it going?" His voice was hushed as his amused gaze eyed her from head to toe. Morgan knew she looked ridiculous with her hair in four different ponytails and the heavily made up face.

"Hey, nice pj's."

She looked down at her oversize pink flannel.

"Sexy, huh?"

"Oh, green eyes, you have no idea." He tugged on one of her ponytails. "I particularly like your lipstick. In fact I need a taste…" He leaned down and covered her mouth with his. The kiss slowly turned heated and when Justin finally broke away, she was dizzy.

"I—I should get back to the girls," she managed to say.

He touched his forehead to hers. "I can't thank you enough for doing this for Lauren." He trailed kisses along her jaw to her neck. He was making a good start, she thought, wrapping her arms around him.

"It's been fun… But you should go, you're in 'no boys' territory." She pulled away again.

"How about a good-night kiss?" he asked.

She raised an eyebrow. "What were we doing?"

"What can I say? I can't get enough of you." He reached for her and she went willingly into his arms. Each kiss only increased her feelings for this man. He made her feel things she hadn't felt in a long time…if ever. Suddenly the sound of giggles broke through her haze.

She jumped back to see the four girls standing in the doorway. "You kissed Lauren's daddy," Delaney said and all the girls nodded in agreement.

Morgan blushed as Justin released her and crouched down to the girls. "That's because I'm the kissing monster… I come out at night looking for pretty girls to kiss." He winked up at Morgan, then turned back. "And it looks like I found some more pretty girls."

The girls screeched and ran back into the room.

Morgan couldn't help but laugh. "I think you better go."

"So, no more kisses, huh?"

"I think you've had enough."

He pulled her to him. "I don't think that's possible." He kissed her nose. "I'm looking forward to having some time with you myself."

"So am I," she admitted.

His eyes grew intense. "Will you come by the house tomorrow? The furniture is going to be delivered."

Morgan heard the giggling voices. "Okay. But I've got to go now."

"Thanks for trusting me, Morgan."

Her heart leaped. "Thank you for being patient."

"All good things are worth the wait—and that definitely includes you."

"I think it finally looks like we're where we want it to be," Justin said as he looked over the blueprints of the future resort on the new drafting table in his home office. The twice-revised model of the hotel was like a dream come true. His dream. His project without his father breathing over his shoulder, without the continual criticisms.

This was his success. His future.

"Well, they say the third time is the charm," Marc Rhodes said. The young project manager had always come through for Hilliard Industries. This time it wasn't any different.

"I can't wait for Morgan to see this."

"Can't wait for me to see what?"

Both men turned to the door as the woman in question walked in.

"Morgan…"

Justin was taken aback seeing her in a black

angora sweater tucked into fitted taupe slacks with a gold belt looped at her tiny waist. Her hair was pulled back into a bun and big hoop earrings adorned her ears. Damn. She looked good.

And Marc noticed her, too.

"Hello, I'm Morgan Keenan," she said as she walked across the room and held out her hand. "You must be Marc Rhodes."

He shook it. "Guilty. It's great to finally meet you, Morgan. After all our phone calls I feel like I know you." He smiled and looked her over appreciatively. "But you're still a surprise."

Justin wasn't happy. Okay, so Marc was a single thirty-one-year-old guy. And women might find him attractive with his sun-bleached hair and easy smile. He just didn't want Morgan to.

"Morgan, come here and see this."

Morgan walked to the desk, eager to take in the completed room. The rich Mediterranean-blue walls were a great contrast with the dark mahogany furniture, but the small model of the resort drew her to the table. The hotel was a rustic structure using logs and cedar shingles. Even though it was a five-story building it still looked as if it belonged in the mountains.

"Oh, Justin, it's perfect. Just what I'd pictured." She was also surprised to feel such deep emotions, but she'd been working on this project a long time.

"We think so, too," he said. "Now, just because the outside looks rustic, but the inside will be anything but… It's five-star all the way."

"I have no doubt it will be," Morgan said. "I can't wait until we get started."

"I also have to say that I'm looking forward to beginning, too," Marc said. "Since the weather has been so mild, we can get all the preliminary work done next week, and if we're lucky, break ground soon after that." He turned to Morgan. "How does that time frame work for you?"

"Fine. Great," she said. "After this weekend my schedule is clear until the first week in December."

"What's this weekend?" Marc asked.

"It's our Western Days celebration. We turn back the clock over a hundred years. There's Miss Kitty's Casino night Friday and on Saturday the Sadie Hawkins dance." Morgan glanced at the project manager's naked ring finger and she got an idea. "If you're going to be around, Marc, you should come. I mean, unless you have to go back to Denver to see your wife, or girlfriend…"

Marc frowned. "No, I don't have either. In fact, I'll need a place to rent here." He glanced at Justin. "I don't want to end up sleeping in the construction trailer."

"Really." This was just too easy, Morgan thought. "I happen to know someone who could help you with the search."

"That would be nice."

"Let me make a call." Morgan reached into her trouser pocket and took out her cell phone. Walking away from the men, she punched in the Realtor's number that was boldly painted on the storefront next to her sister's law office.

The phone was answered on the second ring. "Hutchinson Realty, Kaley Sims."

"Kaley. It's Morgan Keenan."

"Hi, Morgan."

"I need your help," she said. "Justin's project manager, Marc Rhodes, has just arrived in town and he needs a place to live for the next six months or so, and the company will also need office space. I told him you could help."

There was a long silence, then Kaley said, "Tell me he's good-looking and single—and there are no more Keenan sisters around."

Morgan laughed and turned away from the men in the room. "Yes, to all the above," she told her. "Who knows, this could be more than a commission for you."

"Then send him over."

"Will do. Bye." Morgan flipped the phone closed and went back to the men and gave Marc directions to the realty office. "Just ask for Kaley Sims. She'll be able to help you. I also told her you might be interested in office space, too."

"Good idea. We need to start hiring a crew. Thanks, Morgan," Marc said, then looked at Justin. "Do you need anything else from me today?"

"No. Just go and get settled."

Marc nodded. "Then I guess I'll see you around."

"If you're free, come by here for supper," Justin said. "We'll order pizza."

Marc's gaze went to Morgan. "I think you'll be busy."

Justin put his arm around Morgan's shoulders. "You never can tell, you might be, too."

Looking puzzled, the project manager left.

"So," Justin began. "When did you turn into the town matchmaker?"

"I'm the mayor. I was only trying to help out a new resident."

"And Kaley…"

Morgan shrugged. "I think Kaley and Marc just might hit it off."

"You may be right. I know Marc had been in a long relationship. The girl broke his heart. I think it would be good for him to meet someone new."

Smiling, Justin sat down on the edge of the desk and pulled her between his legs. "You know you didn't have to worry about Kaley."

She frowned. "I'm not worried."

"Good, because you're the only woman I want." He kissed her softly. "I did notice that Marc showed a little more than a passing interest in you." He trailed kisses along her jaw to her ear and whispered, "I thought I was going to have to punch him out."

He felt her smile. "He was just being friendly."

He pulled back. "You walked in here and looked like a million bucks." He looked down at her sweater, over the curve of her full breasts. "Damn, you look great," he whispered.

With a breathy gasp, she took a step closer and wrapped her arms around his neck. He hadn't expected such a soft giving away of control, and it sent a wave of pleasure through him as she touched her lips to his.

With a groan, he stood and slowly increased the assault on her mouth, delving deeper with long, lazy strokes. Her breathing rough, she pressed her body against his, causing a torturous friction between them.

Good Lord. This was crazy. He had to stop… before things got out of hand.

He broke off the kiss and looked down to see the desire in her eyes. "Morgan…you're not helping me here. I want you." He cupped her face. "But I don't think you're ready."

He took hold of her hand and smiled at her dazed look. "You can't say we don't throw off sparks." He grew serious. "It's going to happen between us, Morgan, but only when you're ready."

She blinked those big eyes at him. "I've never felt like this, Justin. I never wanted this so much… until you."

He sighed. "That's not helping me cool off, either. But I can't tell you how happy that makes me." He touched her face because he had to. "I've never wanted a woman like I want you."

"Oh, Justin…"

Morgan was having trouble handling the new feelings. The trembling she felt whenever he touched her, along with the deep ache in her stomach that she wanted him to ease.

"I think we should maybe step back from temptation." He stood. "How about I give you a tour of what's been done around the house."

Surprisingly Morgan wanted to pull him back. She wanted to stay in his arms…forever. To have him show her pleasure, have him tell her how she could please him. She felt the sudden heat touch her face, knowing how close they were getting to that next step.

"You're right. I want to see your bedroom…"

He grinned. "I think that could be arranged." He tugged on her arm and escorted her down the hall. Opening the double doors, he stood back.

"Oh, Justin… It's beautiful." Her gaze traveled around the large room. The walls had been painted a mocha color that offset the dark wood furniture. A huge king-size bed with four carved posts had a dark blue comforter covering it. An armoire stood directly across from it and a blue chenille-covered chaise sat next to the fireplace.

"I still need linens, and the drapes haven't arrived yet."

"It looks pretty good considering a few weeks ago the place was a mess. What about Lauren's room?"

"Come, you need to see this." He motioned for her to follow him to the room across the hall. Lauren's bedroom. Morgan peered in to find bright pink walls, softened by off-white furniture.

"Oh, it's so pretty. Lauren will love it." The double bed had a lace canopy and a dust ruffle. The mattress was bare, with new linens still in their packaging. She walked to the shelves that lined the opposite wall. Justin had finished them off with an intricate trim and painted them white.

"So how did I do?" he asked.

She turned to see he was waiting for her approval. "They're perfect. And Lauren will love them because you made them for her."

"You think so? I measured them to fit her doll collection." He crossed the room. "I hung them here so she could see them from her bed." His expression turned sad. "She and her mother had started collecting the dolls a few years ago. I wanted her to have some good memories of that time."

"It's a wonderful thing to do." She walked into his arms because it seemed so natural. So natural to be with this man, to feel his warmth. He'd been so willing to help her overcome her fears, that she never thought much about his problems.

His arms came around her. "I have a lot to make up for. I wasn't around much when Lauren was a baby." He paused. "The problems between her mother and me kept us at odds. It wasn't healthy. Then, when the divorce finally happened and Crystal couldn't cope… I let my in-laws take care of my daughter."

Morgan stepped back. "Justin, we all make mistakes. That doesn't mean you didn't love your daughter. We can't look back. It's now that's important…and the future. You've brought Lauren here, retired from an all-consuming job to put her first. She knows that." She smiled. "There's no doubt she loves you."

"You and your family have been a big help too," he told her.

"It hasn't exactly been a hardship on us." She laughed, but realized how important Lauren had become to the Keenans…all the Keenans. And Justin. How easily it would be to fall in love with father and daughter, then realized she was halfway there already.

The following Friday night, Morgan examined herself in the mirror in the hotel room. Western Days were in full swing and she, along with her family, were working Miss Kitty's Saloon Night.

Morgan had chosen the most modest dress from the 1880's wardrobe, if there was such a thing. An emerald-green satin that had an off-the-shoulder neckline, but the fitted bodice created cleavage she never knew she had. The skirt was gathered and hit her at the knees, revealing a lot of leg. High heels added to her height.

"Are you sure this looks all right?" she asked and when she didn't get an answer, she turned to her sisters.

"You look incredible," Paige said.

"Really?" Morgan couldn't stop thinking about how Justin would react to her outfit. "You sure it's not too much?"

"You're kidding, right?" Paige glanced down at her large belly. "I'm eight months pregnant and dressed as a saloon girl." She grinned. "And Reed will think I'm sexy as hell."

"Men think everything's sexy," Leah added, rubbing her smaller belly of five months.

This was probably the first time Morgan had truly envied her sisters. They were both having babies. A family of her own had always been Morgan's dream.

Maybe it had to do with their own parents' desertion. A strange yearning settled in her stomach at the thought of a little girl like Lauren…and having a man like Justin.

"I bet Justin is going to think you're sexy," Leah said. "I mean, the man can't keep his eyes off you as it is."

Morgan wanted to deny that there was anything between them, but since Lauren had broadcast their kiss, it was futile. The funny thing was, Morgan wanted them to be a couple. And she was a little frightened about how long he would wait for her to get over what happened years ago.

Her biggest fear was she might never be the woman Justin needed, and she would lose him.

Dressed in jeans, a Western shirt and boots, Justin walked around the saloon at the historic Grand Hotel. Ragtime music played on the piano as mixed sounds of winners and losers filled the crowded room.

He carried a stack of chips he'd bought for tonight's gaming, but he didn't care a lot about the gambling as he did about finding Morgan. He knew she had to work at one of the blackjack tables.

He walked past the roulette table to see Kaley Sims taking the bets, and an attentive Marc Rhodes playing the game of chance. He wished the project manager luck and walked on.

At the sound of more commotion, he glanced around and saw a noisy crowd at a table. He went over to find what he'd been looking for. Morgan

Keenan was dressed like he'd never imagined. Wrong. He had imagined it, but only in his dreams. Suddenly his hopes soared. His heart raced as his body stirred with desire.

She looked incredible. Her hair was swept up, exposing her delicate neck and shoulders. The low-cut green dress matched her eyes and showed off an enticing amount of cleavage. He swallowed the sudden dryness in his throat.

A player got up from the table and he moved in before anyone else had the chance. And there were plenty of guys lurking around. He looked at Morgan, but she seemed to be handling all the attention.

He finally caught her eyes.

"Well, hello, stranger." She gathered up the cards and began to shuffle, but her gaze never left his. "You must be new in town."

"Just got here, ma'am."

"So you're thinking about playing a game of chance?"

"I'll try my luck." He slid four chips along the felt table to his spot.

"Good luck," another gambler called. "She's cutthroat."

Justin gave a sideways glance at the guy next to him. "She doesn't look so tough."

"Trust me, son, she's tough when it comes to getting money for this town," the middle-aged man said. He held out his hand. "Hello, I'm Father John Reilly."

A priest. He shook it. "Hello, Father. Justin Hilliard."

"It's a good thing what you're doing for this town…and the people."

"Well, if things work out right, it's money all around."

The priest nodded. "I like that…spreading the wealth and the jobs. Bless you, son."

"Thank you, Father. I could use it."

As Morgan dealt out the first cards, Justin couldn't stop looking at her. The player to his right asked to be hit with another card, then went bust. The second player said he'd hold at seventeen, since the dealer was only showing a six of hearts.

"What about you, stranger?" Morgan smiled. "Looks like you have a decision to make."

Justin managed to steal a glance at his cards. An ace and a two of clubs. "Hit me."

Morgan turned up the six of hearts.

His mind wasn't counting anything as those emerald eyes mesmerized him. He tapped the table again, unable to see or think about anything but Morgan.

The table erupted in cheers. He glanced down to see the two of clubs. With a smile, he leaned back in his chair. "I think I'll stay."

Morgan moved on to the next person. The player stopped at nineteen, then came the dealer's turn. She flipped over her bottom card to reveal another six and the group began cheering for a face card. It must have worked, because she pulled out the Queen of Spades.

"Looks like I busted." Morgan smiled as she paid off the happy winners.

Justin sat for another thirty minutes when Claire Keenan arrived dressed in a black satin dress and a feather in her hair. "It's break time, Morgan."

The group grumbled until Claire took her place behind the table. "Okay, guys. Let's see if you can keep up with Claire." She winked at Justin as he got up to follow Morgan. He took her hand and together they walked through the casino to the buffet line.

He wanted a more private place to greet her, but he knew that she was the mayor tonight and had to be visible for the charity event. And he, too, should meet and greet.

"Are you having fun?" she asked.

"I am now," he whispered against her ear. "But I have this need to kiss this beautiful...sexy blackjack dealer."

Surprisingly Morgan tugged on his arm, and greeting Destiny's citizens along the way, managed to lead him to the other side of the hotel, up a staircase and along the hall to a door. They went inside to find it vacant except for all the extra costumes.

She turned to him and gave him a coy smile. "I usually don't do this sort of thing, mister, but since you're a stranger in town...and all." She stepped into his arms. "We want you to know what a friendly town Destiny is."

Her mouth met his in a searing kiss.

Justin groaned as he tried to let her keep the lead. It was killing him. He wanted her...more and more with each passing day. Her desire was evident, too.

She kissed him like she was drowning, and he was

her lifeline. Her body moved against his as her tongue slid along the length of his. Finally he raised his head to see her flushed face. He dipped down and took another taste of her, once again, then retreated half a step back.

Morgan's eyes fluttered open. "Oh, my."

He moved further away from temptation. "You are lethal, woman." His gaze roamed over her dress and down to her legs. He could imagine, those long, incredible legs wrapped… He quickly shook away the picture.

"We should get back." He headed to the door.

"Justin…is something wrong?"

He turned around to see the beautiful woman, looking half made love to, and he ached to finish what he started.

"God, no. You are…" He reached out to touch her, but pulled back. "It's not you, Morgan, it's me. I want you so much that, if I touch you again I might break my promise."

He watched her take a shuddering breath. "How about if I release you from that promise? What if I say I want you, too?"

CHAPTER NINE

AN HOUR later, they arrived at Justin's place. Morgan thought she'd be nervous, but she wasn't.

She was with this wonderful man.

Morgan had changed out of her costume into a pair of jeans and a light-blue sweater, but she hadn't taken the time to let her hair down or remove her makeup. After she'd seen Justin's smiling face waiting at the bottom of the hotel steps, she was glad.

Lauren was spending the night with Delaney, and Morgan had told her mother that she'd be going with Justin. She didn't offer any more explanation, nor had Claire Keenan asked for one.

Tonight was just for them.

Silently Justin escorted her through the door, where a soft glow from the light in the entry helped them find their way. Hand in hand, they walked up the sweeping staircase to the second floor, and down the hall. Her heart pounded hard as he opened the door to the master suite and flipped on the light, softly illuminating the room.

Morgan glanced around at the new touches he'd added since her last visit. Beige and blue pillows were scattered on the bed. A large beige and wine rug covered the spacious area in front of the fireplace. Justin reached for a remote on the mantel, pushed a button and flames appeared from the gas logs in the hearth.

"Instant atmosphere," Morgan said as she went to the window seat where a long cushion covered the top.

"It also warms up the room."

She didn't need any more heat. The man across from her was warmth enough.

"How about a drink?"

When she nodded, Justin went into the connecting room, then after a few minutes returned with two glasses and a bottle of wine. She took the crystal goblets from him.

"This may help us relax," he said.

"Do you think I need help…?"

He leaned down and placed a soft kiss against her lips. "Maybe not you, but I do." His mouth was inches from hers. "I want to make this special for you, Morgan. Making love isn't just about the act, it's about sharing, and pleasing the other person…" His gaze searched her face. "It's something you've never experienced. As far as I'm concerned, this will be your first time."

She released a long breath. "Oh, Justin…" There was no doubt she was in love with this guy. "I want to please you, too, but…"

He covered her mouth with another kiss, stopping her words. By the time he pulled back, she forgot what else she was going to say.

"This isn't a test, Morgan." He stood back and worked the cork on the already opened bottle, then poured some wine in each glass. "And we have all night."

He set the bottle down on the end table, then returned to her and held up his glass. "To us…"

"To us…"

Justin couldn't take his eyes off her. Morgan had put such trust in him and he prayed he wouldn't let her down.

She sat on the cushion on the window seat as she sipped her wine. "You've added a lot since I was here last."

"Do you like it?" He took the place next to her.

"Yes, I especially like the rug."

"It was delivered this morning. Thank you for directing me to the furniture store in Durango." Why were they talking decorating? He took her hand in his, kissed it and pressed it against his thigh. "I've liked all the ideas you've given me for the house."

"I'm glad I could help." She took another drink, then she looked at him. "This house is special. It's wonderful that you're restoring it this way." Her hand began moving against his leg. "I don't want to talk about the house all night."

"I don't, either." He took the wine from her and put it on the table, then cupped her face. "God, you're beautiful." He reached up and removed the pins from her hair and helped the fiery curls fall to her shoulders. Then he lowered his mouth to hers, and tasted her, mixed with the wine. Sweet. When her sigh escaped into his mouth, suddenly everything shifted speed. He wrapped his arm around her, and with his lips never leaving hers, he lowered her backward onto the seat. He deepened their pleasure when his tongue mated with hers.

When he released her he looked into her eyes, happy to see the desire there. "You okay?"

She nodded and reached up to caress his face. "I'm more than okay."

He groaned. No woman had even gotten inside him like this. He kissed her again…and again until her body arched wanting more. He moved his hand to her waist, slipped under her sweater and began stroking her bare skin.

She shifted under his touch. It was a small movement, but enough to encourage him. He raised his head and watched her as his hands moved upward to cover her breasts.

Morgan couldn't stay still with Justin touching her. She wanted more…so much more.

She boldly tugged at his shirt and, when it wouldn't budge, she popped the snaps on the Western style shirt.

Justin smiled. "So anxious?"

She felt her face redden. "Well, it only seems fair that I get to touch you, too."

"Then why don't I make it easier for you?" He stood and tugged the shirt from his jeans and stripped it off, leaving him bare from the waist up.

Her pulse raced and she sat up as Justin came back to her. He captured her mouth in another kiss, but it wasn't enough, wasn't helping the ache inside her.

She broke off, grabbed the hem of her sweater and yanked it over her head.

For a long time he just stared at her. Then he finally reached out and touched her, cupping her breasts in his hands. She released a sigh and pressed into his palms.

"Perfect… I knew you would be," he breathed as he lowered his head. Brushing kisses along the exposed fullness, he soon began to concentrate on her hardening nipples through the sheer lacy material of her bra. She gasped when he used his fingers to tease her further.

He raised his head. "You like that?"

Morgan could only nod, then with shaky hands she unfastened the front clasp, baring herself for his eyes. "More…please…" She held the back of his head, bringing his mouth to the sensitive tip.

Justin had waited so long for this…to be with Morgan, but he had to take it slow…and easy.

"Gladly." He closed his mouth over the pebbled nub, using his tongue to add to her pleasure. When she cried out and arched her body to bring him closer, he knew he'd succeeded.

He raised his head to find her emerald eyes dark with hunger. He glanced down at her beauty and he nearly shook from need. His hand moved to the snap on her jeans.

"I want you, green eyes. I want to make love to you…but only if you're ready."

She gave him a slow smile and touched his face. "I've wanted you, too. I've wanted this since we spent the night together in the cave."

"I think I've been waiting for you all my life." He took a long breath and released it, then stood and began to tug off her jeans, revealing her long slender legs.

He stood back and took in all her beauty, from her pretty feet, up her long legs, slender hips and delicate waist to her breasts. She was perfect.

Justin drew another breath and released it, telling himself again he needed to go slow. He placed a tender kiss on her lips and lifted her up in his arms.

"I'm going to make love to you, Morgan," he began as he crossed the room to the bed. "I'm going to tease you into a slow burn, then show you a pleasure you never knew could exist between a man and a woman."

He heard her quick intake of breath as he laid her on the cool sheets. With his gaze never leaving hers, he stripped off his jeans, then stood before her, waiting for her to make the final move, showing that she trusted him to not hurt her, trusted him enough to take her to paradise.

When she reached out her hands, he knew that this was a new beginning…for both of them. He climbed into bed beside her and pulled her into his arms.

This was home.

* * *

Morgan felt light on her face and opened her eyes to the rising sun. A smile creased her lips as she recalled last night, and Justin.

She rolled over and found the man in question beside her, sound asleep. He should be tired. They'd been up most of the night, touching…and loving each other…

She smiled, not the least bit ashamed or embarrassed. Why should she be? She was in love with Justin.

She recalled how patient he'd been with her. How he'd let her take the lead…set the pace. And he helped her discover things about her body. As promised, he showed her pleasure she never dreamed possible.

Morgan's thoughts turned to her sisters. No wonder Paige and Leah were always so happy. Now she knew and she could share in their secret.

She turned to the man who was helping to erase all her bad memories and replace them with good ones. His dark hair was mussed and his jaw already showed dark stubble. His lashes were black and long. She wanted to kiss every square inch of his handsome face.

He blinked and opened his eyes. "What's got you so happy this morning?"

She jumped. "Oh, I thought you were asleep."

He wrapped his arm around her waist, drawing her against him. "I think I still am. I have this beautiful naked woman in my bed. This has to be a dream."

She giggled. "No, I'm real."

His hand covered her breast. "I can tell." He smiled. "Good morning, green eyes."

"Good morning."

"You can do better than that." He leaned over her and captured her mouth with his. A slow, lazy kiss quickly turned heated and hungry. How could she want him again?

He tore his mouth away. "That's one powerful kiss."

"You did pretty good yourself."

He brushed the hair away from her face. "I wish we never had to leave here." He made a throaty sound. "I can't seem to get enough of you."

Morgan's heated gaze locked with his. "Oh, Justin...last night was unbelievable. I never thought... it's just that I never realized how beautiful it could be."

"It's not like this with everyone. It has to be the right person. And it has to be about more than just sex. It was definitely more than that for me last night." He kissed her fingertips.

The phone rang, breaking the mood.

He groaned. "I better get that. It might be about Lauren."

Justin turned toward his side of the bed. He was going to get rid of whoever was calling and fast. He grabbed the receiver. "Hello."

"Mr. Hilliard, this is Carlton Burke."

Burke was Marshal Hilliard's right hand man. What was his father up to? "So my father has you calling me now. What does he want this time?"

Justin didn't appreciate being disturbed on a Saturday morning. He glanced over his shoulder to see Morgan was up, had put on her bra and panties and was slipping into her jeans.

"I'm afraid there's bad news, Mr. Hilliard. Your father had a heart attack last night. He's in intensive care at University Hospital."

Justin's chest constricted as he sat up on the side of the bed. His father was never sick. With the receiver between his shoulder and ear, he grabbed his boxers off the floor and slipped them on. "What is his condition?"

"He's stabilized for now, but the doctors are running tests."

His father could die. "Arrange for the plane to fly to Durango. I'll be there in two hours."

Morgan glanced at him as he gave the order. "I'll see you later today," Justin said and hung up the phone.

"You're leaving?" she asked.

"My father had a heart attack last night. I have to go to Denver."

Morgan rushed around the bed and slipped her arms around him. She could see the pain and confusion in his eyes. "Justin, I'm so sorry. How is he?"

"He's stable for now, but I have to go there… today. Damn." He stopped. "I have to take Lauren, too. Darn she'll miss school."

"Justin, she's not going to care as long as she's with you." That's more than what Morgan had. "Do you want me to pack some of her clothes?"

"That would help me…"

Morgan started to walk away, but he pulled her back into his arms. "I don't want to leave you, either, Morgan. This wasn't how I planned today." He drew back and stared at her. "I want this to be just the beginning for us, but I have to be honest…I don't know what's going to happen. This can't be resolved in a few days."

"I know. And I'll be here, waiting." She hugged him, then went off to pack Lauren's clothes.

She would stay here, but she couldn't help but wonder if Justin would make it back to Destiny. He was returning to his old life in Denver. Whether it was his choice or not, he was still leaving her. Why did she feel she was being abandoned again?

The next day the family gathered in the Keenan kitchen for the Sunday meal. All the talk had been about the Sadie Hawkins dance the previous night.

Morgan hadn't attended the dance, not with Justin in Denver dealing with his father's situation. She wished so much that there was a way she could help him get through this. The trip back wouldn't be easy, considering the two had been estranged. Maybe this situation would help them get closer. Or would the long recovery enable his father to convince his son to stay in Denver?

Another part of Morgan wanted to be selfish. She wanted a chance to be with Justin. A chance at the life he'd hinted at yesterday morning. But would that happen now?

"Morgan," Leah called to her. "Have you heard any more news from Justin?"

She shook her head, telling herself that Justin had been too busy dealing with the crisis to phone her. "He said he would be at the hospital while his father went through tests." She tried to hide it, but she was miserable not hearing.

When the kitchen phone rang, her mother picked it up. "Hello, Keenan Inn." She paused and smiled. "Justin, it's good to hear from you. Yes, she's right here. We're all praying for your father." She held out the receiver to Morgan. "I think someone's anxious to talk to you."

"Thanks, Mom." Morgan took the phone, walked into the hall and sat on the carpeted stairway. "Justin."

"You have no idea how much I need to hear your voice. God, I miss you."

Her heart soared. "I've missed you, too."

"I'm sorry I haven't called sooner, but between the hospital and getting Lauren settled in, there hasn't been time, or it was too late last night."

"That doesn't matter, Justin. You can call me anytime." She hesitated, before asking, "How is your father?"

"He's still stable, and they've been running a barrage of tests. It's going to be another day or so before we know."

"That's good news."

"Dealing with my father when he's confined to a hospital bed has not been fun. He's grumpy with everyone."

"That's a good sign, right?"

"It's hard to tell with that man."

"I wish you could come home."

"You don't know how much I wish that, too,"

he said. "But it's not likely. My father's recovery could take quite a while. And it isn't as if there is anyone else who can run the company. At the moment, it's up to me."

Just as quickly as her mood had brightened by his voice, it now sank low at the thought he might not be returning. "What about your father's assistant?"

"I have power of attorney, and I know the operation. My father didn't trust many people. Except me."

She hadn't trusted easily, either. Until Justin. "It makes sense since you were supposed to take over the company someday." She felt like her entire life was starting to crumble. "So I take it Marc will be running the resort project on his own."

"He can do it, Morgan. Nothing has changed on that. I don't want anything to change, especially us. I'm crazy about you. In fact, when things settle down, I want you come to Denver. Once the resort project breaks ground and construction starts, you should have some free time. You could come here and be with me."

"Justin, I can't do that. I have responsibilities as mayor. I take my job seriously."

"I know." He sighed. "I hate even asking you, but I can't walk out on mine, either. Hilliard Industries employs thousands of people, people with families. The stockholders want someone who knows the business."

Justin was asking for something she couldn't give him. Destiny was the only place she'd ever felt she belonged. "I can't move, Justin. I'm sorry…"

"At least think about it, Morgan? Right now, it's the only way we can be together."

She wanted desperately to be the woman he wanted, but she couldn't move into his world. "Let's not talk about this now."

There was a long pause. "I need to get back. I'll try to call you again. Bye, Morgan."

Before she could speak, she heard the click, then the dial tone. It sounded so final. Had she lost Justin?

She returned the phone to the kitchen to find her family all waiting expectantly for news.

"Justin's dad is still in ICU. So Justin won't be back for a while. He's had to take over as CEO for the company."

"For good?" Paige asked.

Morgan shrugged. "I don't know. I don't think Justin knows for sure."

"I'm sorry, Morgan," her sister said. "But I have no doubt he'll be back. He has the resort and his house here."

Morgan didn't want to talk about this anymore. She couldn't share her feelings for Justin. She'd spent so many years hiding them and acting like the big sister that she didn't know how to share her own problems.

"I'm not very hungry, so if you don't mind, I'll pass on supper."

Before anyone could convince her to stay, Morgan grabbed her coat and was out the door. Pulling up her collar, she took off walking down the street, trying to think positively, but her fears prevented it. She traveled several blocks and realized she was at Justin's house.

She'd come to love this place more and more with every little detail Justin had restored. It was the home she'd always wanted, but she realized she didn't care about the structure, without the man. She used the key Justin had given her. She told herself that she was just checking to see that everything was turned off and locked up tight.

She walked through the main floor, seeing the progress. The living room had new crown moldings, and the workmen had replaced the mantel. She continued into the kitchen to find it empty. New cabinets were ordered and scheduled to be installed next week. But no one would be here.

Her heart was breaking, she hurt so bad.

The doorbell rang, bringing Morgan out of her reverie. She went to answer it, wondering if it was Marc, but was surprised to find Father Reilly on the porch.

"Father, what are you doing here?" She stepped aside to let him inside.

The middle-aged priest smiled sadly as he came into the entry. "I've just heard about Justin Hilliard's father. I wanted to come by…"

"Justin is in Denver."

Of course Father Reilly studied her for a moment. "I can see you're worried. Has his father taken a turn for the worse?"

"No. Mr. Hilliard seems to be holding his own.

But Justin will be staying in Denver, indefinitely, to run the family business."

"So your unhappiness has nothing to do with the resort project."

She shook her head. "Justin assures me that his project manager is more than capable of handling the job." The priest was the only person Morgan had confided in about what happened to her in college. "I don't think Justin will come back here."

Father Reilly took her hand and led her to the stairs. They sat down. "It sounds to me like he didn't have much choice."

"He didn't." She felt so many emotions. "It's all happened so fast…"

"And even more for Justin. He's had to pack up his life here and rush back to handle things." The priest paused. "I take it the two of you have feelings for each other."

Morgan thought back to their night together and nodded. "We had just started seeing each other when this happened." She looked at him. "He asked me to move to Denver."

His understanding blue eyes held hers. "And that's a bad thing?"

"I can't leave here, Father. I have commitments to the town, and it's my home. My parents live here."

He watched her for a while. "It's more than that, isn't it, Morgan?" He sighed. "You're still letting what happened to you hold you prisoner, letting it keep you from making a life for yourself."

"I have a life."

"Not a relationship. Have you ever talked with anyone else?"

"Justin knows."

A slow smile appeared across his rounded face. "So you've trusted Justin enough to let him help you with your biggest fear. That's a big step, Morgan. He must be a special man. And a lucky man. I doubt he's going to let a pretty lass like you get away."

CHAPTER TEN

THE next day, Morgan was in her office with Marc, discussing the hiring of local workers. They decided to give the community a head start on the hiring for the project.

"I'll have the office set up by tomorrow." The young project manager smiled. "I have Kaley helping with handing out applications. The construction company will do the screening of the subcontractors…"

The phone rang and Morgan answered it. "Morgan Keenan."

"Good morning, Mayor," Justin said.

"Hello, Justin." She flashed a look at Marc. "How is everything there?"

"Not bad. My father's been moved into a regular room. They found some blockage and plan to correct the problem. How are things there?"

"Busy." Seems he wanted to keep this business. "Marc's here. We're going to begin hiring tomorrow."

"Good. I don't want any delays. Let me talk to him."

She handed the phone to the project manager, telling herself it was better that he hadn't gotten personal. They didn't need that right now. Justin had too much to worry about as it was. On the other hand she couldn't stop thinking about him.

"Okay, Justin. I'll be in touch. Bye." He held out the receiver to her. "He wants to talk to you again."

Surprised, she took the phone and watched as Marc walked out. The door clicked shut, leaving her alone.

"Justin, was there something else you needed?" she asked, her heart beating in double-time.

"Only you, green eyes."

She closed her eyes. "Justin, this isn't a good time." This was only making it worse. "We both have a lot to deal with right now."

"Can't we do it together, Morgan? I think we make a pretty good team."

"It's different now. Your life is different. Your immediate future is there in Denver. Mine is here."

"This is only temporary. My concern is still the Silver Sky project…and you and Lauren."

Morgan bit her trembling lip. "Justin, please, you can't make any promises now. Your life has to be there…"

"We could if we're willing to compromise."

She didn't want to argue with him. "I think we should put this conversation off for a while."

There was a long pause. "If that's what you want."

No! She wanted more than anything to be with Justin, but that wasn't possible right now. Maybe never. "It's probably better for both of us."

"I guess there's nothing more to say."

"I guess not," she said.

There was a long pause and Morgan almost begged him to come back to her, but she couldn't do that. She couldn't make him choose.

"Goodbye, Morgan."

"Goodbye, Justin."

She hung up first, not wanting to hear the final break in the connection that meant the end. She blinked back the tears, knowing if she started she might never stop.

Morgan went back to work for the rest of the afternoon until a commotion disturbed her. Suddenly Lyle Hutchinson barged into her office, with Beverly close behind him. "Sorry, Morgan. He slipped past me."

"It's okay, Bev," she told her, then looked at her intruder. "You need to see me, Lyle?"

He nodded. "And I think you know why."

Morgan motioned for the town controller to leave them alone. "I'm not in the mood for guessing. Maybe you should just tell me."

"Word's out, Morgan, that Hilliard deserted us."

Morgan got up and moved around her desk. "Deserted?"

"Justin Hilliard pulled out. He's gone."

"That's not true. I just talked with Mr. Hilliard this morning, and I assure you, he's not pulling out of the project. Besides, he's signed a contract, and he'd lose his investment."

"I doubt that matters. The man has plenty of money to lose."

Outside of the investment for the resort project, Morgan hadn't paid much attention to Justin's financial worth. "Whether he does or not doesn't concern me. My only concern is that his project manager can handle things here. But I assure you, Mr. Hilliard is in close touch with everything concerning the project."

Lyle gave her a cold stare. "I don't believe you," he said. "I think you're trying to cover for him. And I'm sure the city council would be interested in the situation."

That did it. Something in Morgan snapped. She was so tired of this man dogging her every step, questioning her every move. Lyle Hutchinson had tried everything to discredit her for the past two years. He hadn't succeeded because she hadn't done anything wrong. In fact, she was doing a good job as mayor.

And she wasn't about to let him smear Justin's good name.

"Well, you go and tell the council whatever you want, Lyle," she began, her anger rising. "I'm tired of your threats and accusations." She walked toward him, suddenly feeling empowered. "You're only ticked off because I beat you in the election. Well, get over it, Hutchinson."

The older man actually backed up, but she didn't stop.

"The citizens of Destiny wanted me—not you— as their mayor. And that's because I do things for the good of this town, not to line my own pockets."

His nostrils flared. "How dare you?"

"It's about time someone told you off. You and your father aren't running this town anymore. So stop coming in here thinking you can frighten me into quitting." She drew a breath and placed her hands on her hips, feeling her energy soar. "Okay, Lyle, give me your best shot."

"You can't talk to me that way."

"Looks like I just did." She smiled. "Now, the next time you want to discuss something with me, you call and make an appointment. I'm busy trying to build a ski resort." She was shaking, but refused to back down. She turned and walked to her desk. Surprisingly all she heard was the door opening and Lyle's retreating footsteps.

Suddenly there was a sound of applause. Morgan swung around to see Beverly. "It's about time someone told that man off."

Morgan began to laugh. "Oh, it did feel good." For the first time in years, she felt free. She'd been hiding behind her fears for so long, she hadn't known her own strength.

Then it dawned on her who had made this possible. The man who gave her her freedom so she'd have the courage to go after what she wanted. And she wanted Justin. Nothing else mattered. But first, she needed to get rid of her other demons.

Later that evening, Morgan sat at the Keenan kitchen table. She'd done what Father Reilly suggested and told her parents what had happened with Ryan.

Morgan reached for her mother's hand, knowing that she desperately needed that loving contact now.

Since that first day she and her sisters had arrived here all those years ago, Claire and Tim Keenan had always been there for them. This time wasn't any different.

"I'm sorry, Mom."

"Don't you ever say that—you have nothing to be ashamed of." Claire Keenan leaned closer, unashamed of the tears in her eyes. "This was out of your control, Morgan. I'm only upset because you went through this alone." Her mother continued to study her. "Please, don't tell me you still believe it was your fault."

"In my mind, no…but emotionally I couldn't help thinking that I was flawed in some way."

Her father spoke up. "Your mother or I never saw any flaws in you. From the first day you came to us, you tried so hard to be perfect. You had the cleanest room, did the most chores and were the top student in school. We always worried that you expected too much of yourself."

Morgan knew what they said was true. "I was so happy to be here. And I was scared that you wouldn't love me if I did anything bad." She felt so childish telling them all this now. "My biological mother gave me away… I thought it was something in me that she couldn't love."

A tear ran down her mother's cheek as she and her husband exchanged a look.

"How could we not love you," Tim asked. "We

prayed for years for a child and suddenly we were blessed with three little girls." Her father cupped her cheek. "From the moment I saw you huddled with your sisters…those big green eyes and wild red hair, you stole my heart. You tried to act so brave. I had to tread so carefully…to earn your trust…your love."

Morgan let a tear fall. "I love you both so much."

"Have you told Justin about what happened in college?" her mother asked.

Morgan nodded. "At first I tried to keep him at a distance, but he wouldn't let me." Sadness washed over her. "But I let him down, Mom. I let him down when he needed me the most. I thought I couldn't handle leaving here…it's been my safe place for so long. Then I realized that Justin is my safe place, too. I love him so much."

Her parents both smiled, then her father said, "Tell us something we don't know."

Morgan smiled, too, hoping one day she and Justin would have a relationship like theirs. "I need to tell him how I feel."

"Tell who how you feel?"

Morgan looked up to see Leah and Paige standing in the doorway. Both expectant mothers should be home and in bed at this late hour.

"What are you two doing here?" Morgan asked as she got up from the table.

"Since no one called us with any news," Paige began, "we decided to come to the source. Mom. And we got this feeling that you needed us."

Morgan hurried over to her siblings and they exchanged hugs. Then Leah added, "And we got this feeling that you need someone to tell you to latch onto that guy of yours. Justin Hilliard is a keeper."

Morgan laughed and it felt good. "I guess you better help me go and pack my suitcase, I'm going to Denver."

"You need to set up a meeting with the office staff," Marshal Hilliard told his son. "Then contact the key stockholders to assure them that Hilliard Industries is on solid ground. The list is in my files."

Over the past five days, Justin had promised himself he wasn't going to let his father rile him anymore. It had been forty-eight hours since he'd been released from the hospital, since the doctors had informed him that his father hadn't had a heart attack, but a severe angina condition. Not that it wasn't serious but they had found some blockage that had been handled by a successful angioplasty procedure.

The doctors expected Marsh Hilliard to make a complete recovery in about six weeks. The over-worked CEO still needed to make drastic changes in his lifestyle, but that wasn't going to be at Justin's expense.

Justin paced his father's study, promising himself he would never turn into Marshall Hilliard. He had entirely different plans for his and Lauren's life…and hopefully that included Morgan. And if he was lucky enough to have her in his life, that life wasn't going to be in Denver.

He thought back to the night they'd made love. It had been incredible. Morgan had been so loving and so giving of her body...and her soul. He'd been humbled how easily she put her trust in him. The first man in years. He could still see the look on her face when he left her...

He knew now, coming back here was toxic. How could he ask her to come into this life? That was wrong, especially when there wasn't anything here that he wanted.

God. He had to talk to her. He had to tell her how he truly felt, that he was coming home to her. But not just yet. First, he had to organize things with the company before he could make her any promises.

It wouldn't take long, maybe twenty-four hours. This had affected Lauren, too. She started reverting into her shell. No, this wasn't the place for either of them.

He glanced at his father sitting behind the desk. The man was going over the quarterly figures. He never stopped working. "I'll hold the meeting in the morning, but I'm going to turn things over to Carlton Burke. He's an excellent candidate to take over permanently."

"You can't be serious."

"I'm very serious," Justin said. "The man has worked for you for ten years. He's practically been your shadow."

"He's not my son," Marshal countered. "For three generations a Hilliard has been at the helm of the operations."

"Then you should adopt him."

"Don't be impertinent," his father said.

"Then listen to what I'm saying. I am not running Hilliard Industries now, or ever. I have a new life in Destiny where there's a special woman that I love very much. And if I'm lucky, she'll share my life and Lauren's. We're going to be a family." How he hoped for that. He still needed to convince Morgan.

"Now, if you'll excuse me, I'm going to put Lauren to bed. If you need something, I'm sure your nurse will help you. Good night, Father."

Justin's shoes echoed on the Italian tile floors as he hurried toward the staircase to the second floor. He wanted to call Morgan, to tell her how much he loved her… He paused. He'd never told her. He cursed.

"Oh, Daddy. You said a bad word."

He looked to the top of the stairs to see Lauren dressed in her nightgown with her favorite stuffed animal in her arms.

He smiled. "I'm sorry, sweetie."

"Are you mad at Grandfather again?"

He reached the top step and swung her up in his arms. "Yes, but I shouldn't be because he doesn't feel good."

"He has a bad heart," Lauren said.

"Yeah, he does." In more ways than one, he thought.

"I hope he gets better real soon so we can go back home to Destiny. I miss my friends and school. And Delaney is having a birthday party in two weeks. She's my best friend in the whole world. I got to be there." She laid her head on his shoulder. "And I miss Morgan the most."

"Oh, honey, I miss Morgan, too. And trust me I'm going to try really hard to get us back where we belong." He carried the sleepy child down to her old bedroom and laid her on the bed. He kissed her. "Night, sweetie."

"Night, Daddy. I love you."

"I love you, too." He shut off the light and closed the door. He wasn't waiting any longer. He was returning to Destiny tomorrow. He'd run Hilliard Industries by phone if he had to. He walked to his room and began searching through his desk. He wasn't going back empty-handed, either.

This time he was going to keep his promises to Morgan.

Morgan knew it was late, but she was afraid if she waited until morning she'd lose her nerve and just fly back home. The taxi pulled up in front of the rolling estate. Floodlights lined the long circular driveway as the cab stopped in front of the huge house.

"Oh, my." Her eyes widened as she tried to take it all in. She knew Justin's family was wealthy but she hadn't expected this.

"Hey, lady. You stayin' or what?"

"I'm going in…but please wait for me." She gave him an extra twenty dollars to stay put. What if she came all this way and Justin didn't welcome her with open arms? It had been five days. Maybe his old life had been too strong a temptation. No. She believed he cared about her, but old insecurities were hard to ignore.

Morgan stepped out of the back seat and brushed her hand along her taupe slacks and straightened her black sweater. The outfit that Justin liked so much, hoping his tastes hadn't changed. She walked up the large porch and rang the bell. Her heart pounded loudly in her ears. After waiting several miserable seconds, a woman answered the door.

"I'm here to see Justin Hilliard," Morgan said.

"I'm sorry, Mr. Hilliard has retired for the night. You can leave your name and come back in the morning…"

Her heart sank. "I'm Morgan Keenan."

"The mayor of Destiny?" The housekeeper smiled. "Miss Lauren talks about you and your family all the time." Before Morgan could say any more, the woman ushered her inside. "Now you wait right here," she told her. "Mr. Hilliard just went to put Lauren to bed." The woman ran off.

Morgan glanced around the darkly paneled area and heavy ornate furniture. Original artwork covered the walls, but no family pictures, or flowers. Was this where Justin had grown up? She realized how lucky she'd been having the Keenans.

Now, she just had to let Justin know how much she loved him, whether he lived here or in Destiny.

"Who are you?" a gruff voice called to her.

Morgan swung around to see an older man with thick gray hair and the same silver eyes as his son. He was wearing a dark silk dressing robe and slippers covered his feet.

"Hello, Mr. Hilliard. I'm Morgan Keenan," she said as she held out her hand. "I'm happy to see that you're doing so well."

He ignored her gesture. "You still haven't answered my question, Miss Keenan."

Morgan was taken aback by his rudeness, even if she were in his house. "I apologize for disturbing you, I only came to see—"

"She's here to see me," the familiar voice called from the stairs.

Morgan turned to see Justin. "Justin…" She drew in a breath as she tried to take in the sight of him. He had on jeans and a hunter-green colored sweater. His hair was mussed, and he looked tired…and wonderful.

"Hello, Morgan," he said as he walked toward her. Never taking his eyes from her, he said, "Father, I thought you'd retired for the night."

The older man grumbled something. "As you can see there is a visitor." He looked her over. "It's a little late for business."

"Morgan's visit is personal." Justin placed a protective arm around her waist.

"I'm not here on business, Mr. Hilliard," Morgan told him. "I'm here to see your son, but I do apologize for the late hour."

Justin couldn't believe it when Nancy had come to him and said Morgan was here. He couldn't get down the stairs fast enough.

"Father, Morgan and I have matters to discuss."

The older man stared at Morgan. "You're not

going to talk my son into leaving here. His place is running Hilliard Industries."

"I know, Mr. Hilliard. That's why I came here." She turned to Justin and smiled. "I want your son to know that I'll support any decision he makes, whether it's here in Denver, or back in Destiny."

Justin didn't want to have this conversation in front of his father. "Father, if you'll excuse us, I need to talk with Morgan…in private."

As if he'd arranged it, the hired nurse arrived and escorted the older man out, but not without some more grumbling. Then all at once there was silence.

Justin's gaze roamed over her face. She was so beautiful. Her hair brushed her shoulders in curls, so soft he ached to touch them. "I can't believe you're here."

"I can't believe it, either," she said timidly. "You really don't mind?"

Justin lowered his head and, inches from her mouth, he said, "Does this seem like I mind?" He covered her mouth with a searing kiss. By the time he released her, they were both struggling to breathe. "This has been the longest five days in my life. God, I've missed you." He kissed her again…and again.

"You're starting to convince me," she teased.

"Well, the last thing I want to do is leave you with any doubt…" He pulled her against his body. "I want you to know exactly how I feel about you." He gazed into those sparkling eyes. "I love you, Morgan Keenan…with all my heart."

She gasped. "Oh, Justin, I love you, too. I'm sorry I told you I wouldn't come to Denver… I was afraid."

"Afraid of what? Me?"

"No. That I wouldn't fit in here. That you were going to come back and decide you wanted the life you had before. And if that's what you really want…"

He placed a finger over her mouth. "No, I don't want anything from my old life, except for Lauren. In the last five days, I realized how much I missed you and Destiny. I consider it my home now. What I didn't expect to find was you." He cupped her face. "I think I fell in love with you in the cave that night. But I knew to win you, I'd have to be patient. I had to get you to trust me. We have nothing without trust."

She nodded. "I know. And I'm sorry it took me so long to realize that. I couldn't trust your love until I trusted myself." She lowered her eyes. "That's why I came here…to you."

Justin had thought of so many things he wanted to say, but suddenly he was speechless. Everything he'd ever dreamed of was right here. "I need to make a phone call."

She blinked. "Now?"

"Believe me, it's important. You'll understand in a few minutes." He drew his cell phone from his pocket and punched in the numbers. He waited, then heard, "Hello, Keenan Inn."

"Hello, Tim, it's Justin."

"Justin, it's good to hear from you. Is everything okay?"

"Yes, it's very okay. Morgan is here with me." His

arm tightened around her as he took another breath. "I love her very much, sir, and would like to ask your and Claire's permission for Morgan's hand in marriage?"

He heard Morgan's gasp, but couldn't look at her.

"I have to say I'm not surprised. Morgan is a special woman." There was another pause. "You have our blessing, son. Tell Morgan we love her very much, and we'll talk later. Goodbye."

"Thank you. Goodbye." He set the phone down on the table and looked at the woman he loved more than he'd thought possible.

"I'd already decided I was leaving Denver and coming home to Destiny…and you. I realized that nothing is more important than us being together." He reached into his pocket and pulled out an antique ring.

"I never dreamed I'd find someone like you. Someone who made me feel…the way that you make me feel…someone who wants the same things." He held up an antique emerald ring circled by diamonds and saw the hue mirror in her eyes. "This was my grandmother's, and I think it's perfect for you."

Never breaking eye contact, he knelt down on one knee. "Morgan Keenan, I love you. Will you do me the honor of marrying me and becoming my wife and mother to Lauren, and more children?"

Morgan all but stopped breathing. Tears flooded her eyes and she could barely see him, but she knew her answer. "Oh, Justin, yes, I'll marry you."

He immediately slipped the ring on her finger,

then stood up and pulled her into his arms. "I want to give you the world."

She pulled back and smiled. "You already have. You helped me find me." He'd given her what mattered the most. "I love you, Justin Hilliard." She kissed him.

"Daddy, you're kissing Morgan…"

They broke apart to see Lauren climbing down the steps. "Morgan, you came to get us." The child rushed into her arms.

"Yes, I did," Morgan said as she knelt down. "And I'm going to take you and your daddy back home to Destiny."

Those big blue eyes widened. "Really?" She glanced up at her father.

"And there's more news, sweetie." He picked her up in his arms. "Your daddy and Morgan are going to get married."

"Oh, boy! Delaney said you would because you guys kiss so much."

"How do you feel about Morgan being your new mother?"

She nodded. "I want that the most." She turned to Morgan and kissed her. "I love you, Morgan."

Morgan hugged her new daughter. "I love you, too." She suddenly understood what her parents had been trying to tell her. You didn't need to give birth to a child to love her.

Lauren straightened. "And can we have sleep-overs?"

Morgan fought laughter. "We'll see, but right now

you need to go to bed. We have to go home tomorrow."

"Yeah. Can I see Delaney, too?"

"Sure."

The five-year-old wiggled out of her arms and got down. "You have to take me to bed, Morgan. Come on, I'll show you how to do it…"

Morgan looked back at Justin who shrugged. "I guess you should learn the ritual." He'd started after them when there was a knock at the door. Justin opened the door to find the cabdriver.

"Oh, my, I forgot about him," Morgan said. "I had him wait in case…"

Justin pulled out some bills and paid the driver handsomely for looking after her. Then he took her bag and followed the girls up the steps.

When they got to the top of the stairs, Lauren said, "Maybe Morgan can sleep in my bed tonight?"

Morgan glanced at the hopeful look on the child's face. "How about I stay with you until you fall asleep?"

"I like that." The girl walked ahead of her parents and into the bedroom.

"Welcome to parenthood. Be careful, she'll steal your heart."

Morgan looked at the man with the silver eyes. "Why not, her father already has." She kissed him. "But I think my heart is big enough to go around."

He hugged her. "How did I get so lucky?"

"It must have been the sweet proposal I sent that lured you to Destiny."

He grinned. "Oh, yeah, and I seem to remember something about some fringe benefits you promised me."

She winked. "I'll discuss those terms later…when we're alone."

EPILOGUE

IT TURNED out to be a perfect day for a wedding.

The mid-December morning had produced a dusting of snow for the noontime nuptials that had been performed by Father Reilly at St. Andrews Church. Since Morgan couldn't choose, both her sisters, Paige and Leah, acted as her matrons of honor, along with Lauren as the flower girl.

It was a holiday theme, but with hundreds of white roses trimmed with silver ribbon. The girls wore winter-green dresses. But when Morgan walked down the aisle on her father's arm, she wasn't seeing anything but her groom standing at the altar. Justin looked handsome in his dove-gray morning coat. There were tears in both their eyes when they'd changed their vows, then he drew her in his arms as Father Reilly pronounced them man and wife.

"Hello, Mrs. Hilliard," Justin whispered then he kissed her with a promise of life filled with love.

The reception had been held at the Inn where

family and friends toasted them in their new life together. Finally by midevening—with Lauren staying with her new grandparents—Morgan and Justin were about to escape the party.

Although the honeymoon had been delayed until after the holidays and Paige giving birth, they had their own special plans.

A thrill raced though Morgan as Justin opened the door to the newly remodeled Hilliard home. He swung her up in his arms and carried her over the threshold.

"Welcome home, Mrs. Hilliard," he whispered as he brought her into their new home and their new beginning. He set her down and kissed her, slow and deep.

"Very impressive welcome, Mr. Hilliard."

"You're the one who's impressive…and beautiful," he said as he eyed her hungrily.

"Thank you."

Morgan wore her grandmother's ivory wedding dress. The antique lace over satin had a fitted bodice with scalloped edging just above her breasts, with long, tapered sleeves that ended in a v-point at her wrist. The trim waistline flared into an A-line skirt that went all the way to the floor.

He pulled her back into his arms. "It's a beautiful dress, but I can't wait to get you out of it."

A shiver went through her as he kissed her, then they walked up the stairs to their bedroom.

Justin wanted everything to be so special since their honeymoon had been put on hold until after the first of the year. That was all right with him as long as he could spend some time alone with his new bride, and he didn't care where.

He opened the bedroom door to expose the lit candles, a fire going and a chilled bottle of champagne beside the bed.

She walked around the room, touching all the flowers. "Oh, Justin. It's...beautiful."

"I had a couple of elves come in. I wanted tonight to be special for you."

She came back to him and slipped her arms around his waist. "Just being with you is all I need. You made it all possible. No one has ever been so patient...so giving with me. You helped me become the woman I always wanted to be."

"No, Morgan. You were always that woman. You just needed someone to help you find her."

She rewarded him with a bright smile. "Well, you've got her now."

He kissed the end of her nose. "That was my plan from the moment I first saw you. You saved me, too. I've never felt this way about anyone... ever."

"I feel the same way about you." She placed her hand against his chest, right over his heart. "I want to give you a part of me that I've never shared with anyone else."

Justin remembered their first time together. How her faith and trust in him had humbled him. "That night was so special to me, to us, and we're going to have many more. Starting tonight." He kissed her.

She broke it off. "There's something I have for you."

His eyes searched hers. "You're all I need, Morgan."

She smiled. "And you're all I need. But I want to carry on tradition. Besides, we can share this gift." She went to the large chest at the foot of the four-poster bed, knelt down, opened it and took out a large quilt.

Justin went to her and examined the multiblue colors displayed in the pattern. "This is the one you were quilting the day I met you." He knelt down beside her, his fingers tracing the intricate pattern of circles.

She nodded. "It's called a wedding-ring quilt. Lauren helped me with some of the stitches, and in the last few weeks, Paige, Leah and my mom helped me finish so it would be ready for today." She looked at him. "For a long time, I'd never thought I'd ever sleep under a wedding-ring quilt."

He shook his head. "I'm just glad you waited for me, too." He pulled her closer as his mouth covered hers. She melted into him at once, her arms snaked around his neck as she opened her lips, welcoming him into a deeper intimacy.

"I love you, Justin," Morgan said as she began to work the studs on his shirt.

"And I love you, Morgan Keenan Hilliard."

He kissed her again, eager to start the honeymoon. He also knew that he needed to pace things, to make everything perfect for his bride on their wedding night. "Why don't you go and take off your gown? I'd hate for anything to happen to it.

Who knows, maybe Lauren or one of our other daughters will want to wear this dress on her wedding day."

He saw the tears as he helped his bride to her feet, then with a soft kiss, turned her around and began working the many buttons down the back. He took several calming breaths as he exposed his wife's slender back.

"All finished," he said and placed a kiss against her neck.

Morgan turned around, holding the loosened dress to her breasts. She raised her loving gaze to his. "I want a baby, Justin. Your baby."

His chest tightened. They'd been so busy getting the wedding together and the project started, they hadn't talked much about children…

"You want a baby…now?"

She nodded. "I know we have the resort project and Lauren needs to adjust to us, but all I can think about is how much I want to be pregnant with your child."

His mouth went dry with the image of her large with his baby. It was so overwhelming he couldn't speak. He pulled her into his arms and kissed her. In no time her dress was removed, then his clothes began to fade away as they found their way to the bed. No words needed to be spoken as he lowered her to the mattress. "I'd love a little girl with your green eyes…" He bent down and brushed a kiss against her mouth, then down her neck, continuing the trail along her sensitized skin.

"Or…" Morgan sucked in a breath. "A little boy with silver eyes and dark curly hair would be… perfect."

"You're perfect…" His mouth returned to hers in a deep, soul-searching kiss that nearly drove him over the edge as his arms tightened, pulling her against his heated body.

They were lost in each other when suddenly the phone next to the bed rang. Justin groaned as he rolled away from his bride. "I can't believe this." Justin grabbed the receiver. "This better be an emergency."

"I'm sorry, Justin. It's Tim. We just wanted to call and let you know that Paige went into labor. She's on the way to the hospital. We've taken Lauren over to Delaney's house for the night. I thought you and Morgan would want to know."

"Of course, Tim. Thanks for the call. I'll tell Morgan."

Morgan sat up in bed, the sheet pulled up to cover her nakedness. "Who was that?"

"Your dad. Paige is in labor and on the way to the hospital."

A smile appeared. "She's having the baby." She let the sheet drop. "I guess Mom will call us with the news."

Justin was getting his first lesson on family, and how important it was to be together. "I guess we better get dressed so we can go welcome the new addition to the family."

"But what about our honeymoon?"

"It's also our family…and Paige is having a baby. She needs you there." He leaned closer and kissed his bride. "I'm never going to come between you and your sisters. I know how close you are."

"Oh, Justin," she said. "I love you so much."

He grinned. "Oh, yeah? I guess you'll just have to show me how much when we get back home."

An hour later, Morgan and Justin rushed into the hospital waiting room where her father and Holt sat. "Where are Mom and Leah?"

"They're in with Paige and Reed," Tim said. "Go on in. Even though she asked us not to call you, your sister wants you here. Room 304."

Morgan kissed Justin. "I'll be back with some news. Thanks for this…"

"This is important, we'll have our time later."

"Later," she whispered. She took off down the hall where Reed was coaching Paige through a pain and Mom and Leah were encouraging her. When it passed, Morgan walked into the room.

"I hear my niece is going to make an appearance today."

"Morgan!" Paige held out her hands. "I told them not to disturb your honeymoon."

"And I'd never forgive you," Morgan said as she went to her sister. "You can't have this baby without your big sister here. Remember, we always stick together."

There were tears in Paige's eyes. "Always. But I wish she'd hurry up."

"Me, too," Morgan agreed. "Then little Ellie can share her birthday with our anniversary."

Paige and Reed had decided to name their daughter after the sisters' biological mother. Eleanor Bradshaw. There were tears in Paige's eyes.

Another pain gripped Paige, and Morgan took her sister's hand and helped her through the breathing. When it passed, Reed fed his wife some ice chips.

"I bet this wasn't how Justin planned to spend tonight," Reed teased.

"Don't worry about Justin," Morgan told him. "I'll make it up to him."

Suddenly realizing what she'd said, Morgan's face reddened but another labor pain drew her immediate attention.

Over the next hour things progressed rather quickly. And in the end, it was the doctor, a nurse and Paige and Reed who were in the room when their daughter arrived into the world.

At the sound of the vigorous cry, Justin squeezed Morgan closer to his side. Then Reed came out with a big grin and tears in his eyes. "Eleanor Claire is healthy and weighed in at six pounds eight ounces and twenty inches long. And she's just as beautiful as her mother."

Everyone cheered, then quietly filed into the room to see Paige beaming, looking too good for just having a baby.

Justin held Morgan close as they looked at the new addition to the family. A precious little girl. They seemed to run in the Keenan family.

Morgan and Leah gathered at Paige's bedside, exchanging hugs while Reed and Holt stood next to Justin. "They've always been close," Holt remarked. "And marriage hasn't changed anything."

They turned their attention to the infant in the crib. "Congratulations, Dad," Justin said. "She's a guaranteed heartbreaker."

"Like her mother and her aunts," Reed agreed.

Reed looked at Justin. "If I hadn't said it yet, welcome to the family."

"Thank you, but I think you've been a little busy." Justin glanced at his wife across the room. As if she sensed his gaze, she turned to him and smiled. She said something to her sisters. They hugged and she came to him.

"We should go," she whispered.

Justin didn't have to be asked twice. They said their goodbyes to everyone and walked out the door. At the elevator they waited until the doors opened and they stepped inside the empty car.

When the door closed Justin pulled his wife into his arms and kissed her. When he broke away, he refused to release her.

She smiled. "Wow. You sure you can wait until we get home?"

He took a breath. "I am home. Whenever I'm with you."

Her green eyes searched his, showing her emotions. "Oh, Justin, I feel the same way. I'm so happy that you didn't give up on me."

He kissed her again. "Never. I would have waited for you as long as it took to win you."

She touched his cheek. "The wait is over, Justin."

"For both of us. We have our family." Who knew, when he'd come here just months ago, he'd find his true Destiny.

* * * * *

THE ROYAL HOUSE OF NIROLI
Always passionate, always proud

The richest royal family in the world—united by
blood and passion,
torn apart by deceit and desire

Nestled in the azure blue of the Mediterranean Sea, the
majestic island of Niroli has prospered for centuries.
The Fierezza men have worn the crown with passion
and pride since ancient times. But now, as the king's
health declines, and his two sons have been tragically
killed, the crown is in jeopardy.

The clock is ticking—a new heir must be found
before the king is forced to abdicate. By royal decree
the internationally scattered members of the Fierezza
family are summoned to claim their destiny. But any
person who takes the throne must do so according to
The Rules of the Royal House of Niroli. Soon secrets
and rivalries emerge as the descendents of this ancient
royal line vie for position and power. Only a true
Fierezza can become ruler—a person dedicated to their
country, their people…and their eternal love!

*Each month starting in July 2007,
Harlequin Presents is delighted to bring you
an exciting installment from*
THE ROYAL HOUSE OF NIROLI,
*in which you can follow the epic search
for the true Nirolian king.
Eight heirs, eight romances, eight fantastic stories!*

Here's your chance to enjoy a sneak preview of the
first book delivered to you by royal decree…

FIVE minutes later she was standing immobile in front of the study's window, her original purpose of coming in forgotten, as she stared in shocked horror at the envelope she was holding. Waves of heat followed by icy chill surged through her body. She could hardly see the address now through her blurred vision, but the crest on its left-hand front corner stood out, its *royal* crest, followed by the address: *HRH Prince Marco of Niroli…*

She didn't hear Marco's key in the apartment door, she didn't even hear him calling out her name. Her shock was so great that nothing could penetrate it. It encased her in a kind of bubble, which only concentrated the torment of what she was suffering and branded it on her brain so that it could never be forgotten. It was only finally pierced by the sudden opening of the study door as Marco walked in.

"Welcome home, *Your Highness*. I suppose I ought to curtsy." She waited, praying that he would laugh and tell her that she had got it all wrong, that the envelope she was holding, addressing him as Prince Marco of Niroli, was some silly mistake. But like a tiny candle flame shivering vulnerably in the dark, her hope trembled fearfully. And then the look in Marco's eyes extinguished it as cruelly as a hand placed callously over a dying person's face to stem their last breath.

"Give that to me," he demanded, taking the envelope from her.

"It's too late, Marco," Emily told him brokenly. "I know the truth now…." She dug her teeth in her lower lip to try to force back her own pain.

"You had no right to go through my desk," Marco shot back at her furiously, full of loathing at being caught off-guard and forced into a position in which he was in the wrong, making him determined to find something he could accuse Emily of. "I trusted you…."

Emily could hardly believe what she was hearing. "No, you didn't trust me, Marco, and you didn't trust me because you knew that I couldn't trust you. And you knew that because you're a liar, and liars don't trust people because they know that they themselves cannot be trusted." She not only felt sick, she also felt as though she could hardly breathe. "You are Prince Marco of Niroli…. How could you not tell me who you are and still live with me as intimately as we have lived together?" she demanded brokenly.

"Stop being so ridiculously dramatic," Marco demanded fiercely. "You are making too much of the situation."

"*Too much?*" Emily almost screamed the words at him. "When were you going to tell me, Marco? Perhaps you just planned to walk away without telling me anything? After all, what do my feelings matter to you?"

"Of course they matter." Marco stopped her sharply. "And it was in part to protect them, and you, that I decided not to inform you when my grandfather first announced that he intended to step down from the throne and hand it on to me."

"To protect me?" Emily nearly choked on her fury. "Hand on the throne? No wonder you told me when you first took me to bed that all you wanted was sex. You *knew* that was the only kind of relationship there could ever be between us! You *knew* that one day you would be Niroli's king. No doubt you are expected to marry a princess. Is she picked out for you already, your *royal* bride?"

* * * * *

Look for THE FUTURE KING'S PREGNANT
MISTRESS
by Penny Jordan in July 2007,
from Harlequin Presents,
available wherever books are sold.

Romantic
SUSPENSE

**Sparked by Danger,
Fueled by Passion.**

Mission: Impassioned

A brand-new miniseries begins with

My Spy

By *USA TODAY* bestselling author

Marie Ferrarella

She had to trust him with her life....
It was the most daring mission of Joshua Lazlo's
career: rescuing the prime minister of England's
daughter from a gang of cold-blooded kidnappers.
But nothing prepared the shadowy secret agent
for a fiery woman whose touch ignited something
far more dangerous.

My Spy

#1472

Available July 2007 wherever you buy books!

Do you know a real-life heroine?

Nominate her for the Harlequin More Than Words award.

Each year Harlequin Enterprises honors five ordinary women for their extraordinary commitment to their community.

Each recipient of the Harlequin More Than Words award receives a $10,000 donation from Harlequin to advance the work of her chosen charity. And five of Harlequin's most acclaimed authors donate their time and creative talents to writing a novella inspired by the award recipients. The More Than Words anthology is published annually in October and all proceeds benefit causes of concern to women.

HARLEQUIN

More Than Words™

For more details or to nominate a woman you know please visit
www.HarlequinMoreThanWords.com

THE GARRISONS

A brand-new family saga begins with

THE CEO'S SCANDALOUS AFFAIR

BY ROXANNE ST. CLAIRE

Eldest son Parker Garrison is preoccupied running
his Miami hotel empire and dealing with his recently
deceased father's secret second family. Since he has
little time to date, taking his superefficient assistant
to a charity event should have been a simple plan.
Until passion takes them beyond business.

Don't miss any of the six exciting titles in
THE GARRISONS continuity, beginning in July.
Only from Silhouette Desire.

THE CEO'S SCANDALOUS AFFAIR

#1807

Available July 2007.

REQUEST YOUR FREE BOOKS!
2 FREE NOVELS PLUS 2
FREE GIFTS!

HARLEQUIN ROMANCE

From the Heart, For the Heart

YES! Please send me 2 FREE Harlequin Romance® novels and my 2 FREE gifts. After receiving them, if I don't wish to receive any more books, I can return the shipping statement marked "cancel." If I don't cancel, I will receive 4 brand-new novels every month and be billed just $3.57 per book in the U.S., or $4.05 per book in Canada, plus 25¢ shipping and handling per book and applicable taxes, if any*. That's a savings of over 15% off the cover price! I understand that accepting the 2 free books and gifts places me under no obligation to buy anything. I can always return a shipment and cancel at any time. Even if I never buy another book from Harlequin, the two free books and gifts are mine to keep forever.   114 HDN EEV7 314 HDN EEWK

Name	(PLEASE PRINT)	
Address		Apt.
City	State/Prov.	Zip/Postal Code

Signature (if under 18, a parent or guardian must sign)

Mail to the Harlequin Reader Service®:
IN U.S.A.: P.O. Box 1867, Buffalo, NY 14240-1867
IN CANADA: P.O. Box 609, Fort Erie, Ontario L2A 5X3

Not valid to current Harlequin Romance subscribers.

Want to try two free books from another line?
Call 1-800-873-8635 or visit www.morefreebooks.com.

* Terms and prices subject to change without notice. NY residents add applicable sales tax. Canadian residents will be charged applicable provincial taxes and GST. This offer is limited to one order per household. All orders subject to approval. Credit or debit balances in a customer's account(s) may be offset by any other outstanding balance owed by or to the customer. Please allow 4 to 6 weeks for delivery.

Your Privacy: Harlequin is committed to protecting your privacy. Our Privacy Policy is available online at www.eHarlequin.com or upon request from the Reader Service. From time to time we make our lists of customers available to reputable firms who may have a product or service of interest to you. If you would prefer we not share your name and address, please check here. ☐

HR07

Coming Next Month

#3961 THE COWBOY'S SECRET SON Judy Christenberry

With one glance Nick Logan knows Abby's little boy is his son, and now he wants the chance to be a father to Robbie. But living with Nick on his Wyoming ranch is more than Abby bargained for. As is the sneaking suspicion that she's never really gotten over the charismatic cowboy.

#3962 THE LAZARIDIS MARRIAGE Rebecca Winters
9 to 5

Party-girl heiress Tracey is determined to show she has what it takes to run her family's empire. Old friend and Greek billionaire Nikos Lazaridis agrees to help—but he's taking her back to basics! Working side by side under the Greek sun, the sparks of attraction are fanned into life!

#3963 THE FORBIDDEN BROTHER Barbara McMahon

Laura Parkerson's life is turned upside down by Jed Brodie. Not just because he is broodingly handsome…but because Jed is her ex-fiancé's twin. He's nothing like his brother, but how can she be sure she's not just bewitched by the mirror image of a man she once loved?

#3964 BRIDE OF THE EMERALD ISLE Trish Wylie

Garrett Kincaid can help beautiful stranger Keelin unlock the secrets of her past. But he won't give her his heart. Except the Irish isle of Valentia is capturing Keelin's imagination and giving her the courage to claim a future. A future that belongs to this man.

#3965 HER OUTBACK KNIGHT Melissa James

As the sun rises in the Outback, two people drive through the silent land, sharing the beauty unfolding around them. They only have eyes for one another. Danni and Jim's journey started as a quest to find the truth, but they soon realize that this journey may really be one of the heart.

#3966 BEST FRIEND…FUTURE WIFE Claire Baxter

Della has always been in love with childhood friend Luke, but Luke's only ever wanted to be friends. Della must make an agonizing decision—reveal her true feelings to Luke and risk rejection, or keep them hidden forever, never knowing what they could have had.

HRCNM0607